A World At Risk

Jochanan Stenesh

BENNINGTON, VERMONT
2016

First published in 2016 by the Merriam Press

First Edition

Book design by Ray Merriam

ISBN 9781576385029
Library of Congress Control Number: 2016906033
Merriam Press #F4-P

This work was designed, produced, and published in
the United States of America by the

Merriam Press
133 Elm Street Suite 3R
Bennington VT 05201

E-mail: ray@merriam-press.com
Web site: merriam-press.com

The Merriam Press publishes new manuscripts on historical subjects, especially military history and with an emphasis on World War II, as well as reprinting previously published works, including reports, documents, manuals, articles and other materials on historical topics.

Contents

Preface

ALBERT Einstein is alleged to have said "I know not with what weapons World War III will be fought, but World War IV will be fought with sticks and stones." Thankfully, a catastrophic World War III has not broken out so far. However, few would disagree that the danger of it erupting has grown with the advent of the 21st century. Nuclear saber rattling by North Korea, continued nuclear stand-off between India and Pakistan, Iran's relentless march toward the bomb, and a mounting threat of nuclear material falling into the hands of radical Islamic terrorists — these are all dangerous omens not to be taken lightly.

As if this were not perilous enough, the world is in additional turmoil in many places and for diverse reasons. War is raging in Afghanistan, Iraq, and Syria. An undeclared war is ongoing between Russia and Ukraine. The early euphoria of the Arab Spring has faded and the drive for freedom has been replaced by chaos and violence. The centuries-old animosity between Sunni and Shia has exploded into a violent, hate-driven clash that has set the Middle East on fire. Barbaric Sunni jihadists poured out of Syria into Iraq. Calling themselves the Islamic State of Iraq and Syria (ISIS), they are determined to establish a Caliphate in the territory conquered by them.

Europe is struggling with a large Muslim immigrant community that is not assimilating into host cultures. Additionally, the continent is being overrun by a flood of refugees from Syria and Iraq. Europe's right-wing parties are gaining alarming strength and with it has come a resurgence of anti-Semitism.

In the United States of America, the undisputed leader of the free world and the beacon of Western civilization, the government is in virtual paralysis. Communication between the White House and Congress is poor. In the Congress itself, Republicans and Democrats are polarized to such an extent that very little gets enacted. And the country is rife with ideological and cultural fights, be it about abortion, separation of church and state, evolution, school vouchers, or climate change.

Adding to this mix of man-made calamities the havoc inflicted by natural disasters might well lead one to conclude that the world is truly at risk. And one might wonder what the future bodes for mankind and its planet.

This book of political fiction takes the reader into an imagined future by describing what might happen in the world in the next two decades. Specifically, the future is viewed via twenty-one newspaper dispatches that cover flash points and controversial issues around the globe. The dispatches were written by bureau chiefs of the paper over the period 2020 - 2040.

To Our Readers

AS you know, *World View*—our award-winning Sunday series—was inaugurated on January 19, 2020. The dispatches from around the world were written by our veteran bureau chiefs: Michael Burns, *New York, NY*; Harold Nelson, *London, UK*; and James Morrison, *Sydney, Australia*. The series has enjoyed a wide and loyal readership. Over the years, many of you have asked for reprints of specific articles and quite a few have voiced the wish to see a selection of articles become available in book form. We appreciate your complimentary feedback and are pleased to offer you a selection of *World View* articles in book form at this time. The book is titled *A World at Risk* and the articles were published at different times over a period of twenty years (2020-2040). We trust that you will find them as interesting, provocative, and yes, even relevant, as when they first appeared in print.

Sincerely,
THE EDITORS
The Daily Independent Courier

March 18, 2041

On High Alert

WORLD VIEW

By James Morrison

May 17, 2020

AMMAN, Jordan—Three weeks ago, Iran conducted its first nuclear test. What the UN, the United States, and Israel had all vowed would never happen, namely that Iran would be allowed to possess nuclear weapons, has taken place. The specter of a country led by religious fanatics and having nuclear arms has now become reality.

Reaction of the international community was predictable. The Security Council met in an emergency session and passed a tersely-worded resolution which condemned Iran for having violated the agreement it had solemnly signed with the big six powers (United States, France, Germany, China, Russia, and Britain) in 2015. The United States issued a stern warning putting Iran on notice that any further tests and/or uses of nuclear bombs or warheads might trigger a military response by the United States and other signatories to the agreement. Unfortunately, considering the past record of ineffective UN declarations and of United States threats that were never acted upon, there is little hope that these verbal declarations will have any effect on Iran's future plans. The International Atomic Energy Agency (IAEA) also met in an emergency session. The chair bemoaned the fact that for the last nine months Iran had made the inspections virtually impossible by placing obstacle after obstacle in the inspectors' path. Had that not been the case, the chair stressed, inspectors might have been able to give the international community better advance warning about Iran's break-out steps toward the bomb. But that was all water over the dam.

*

If anyone had entertained any doubts about Iran's willingness to flex its muscle once it acquired nuclear capability, they were quickly disabused of this illusion. In the week following the nuclear test, Iran carried out extensive naval exercises in the Persian Gulf and launched two intercontinental ballistic missiles into the Arabian Sea. No sooner were these maneuvers completed then Iran conducted a Blitzkrieg into southern Iraq. Iran claimed that the lives of the Shia, Iran's coreligionists in that part of Iraq, had reached an intolerable level of danger from the advancing Sunni ISIS in the north. Hence, Iran felt called upon to come to their rescue by entering the area to provide a protective shield. These pronouncements—borrowed from Russia's handbook on its invasion of Ukraine in 2014—were advanced to provide a "moral" justification for the incursion. After four days, Iran had established full control over the southern, densely-populated section of the Tigris/Euphrates river system. The triangular area, known as the Tigris/Euphrates Delta or TE-Delta, extends some 150 miles northwest from the triangle's vertex at the Persian Gulf to the triangle's base (about 150 miles wide) south of Baghdad. The area is bordered on the east by Iran and on the west by the Syrian desert. It had absorbed a large influx of Shia from central and northern Iraq who sought refuge in the south from the brutal ISIS rule in the north. Having accomplished its goal, Iran promptly proceeded to formally annex the area. All remonstrations from the international community were simply ignored.

The ominous message of this series of actions was clear and was not lost on Iran's other neighbors. Israel immediately raised the level of alertness for its military and called up large numbers of the country's reserves. Saudi Arabia and Jordan also beefed up their military preparedness. Even if Iran does not employ its new arsenal at this time, the door has been opened to an arms race in the Middle East. Other countries will likely embark on their own nuclear programs to counter the increased threat from Iran's Mullahs. With these developments, the Middle East has become a virtual powder keg, ready to blow up at the slightest provocation.

*

How did all this come about? The much-touted 2015 agreement between the big six powers and Iran turned out not to have been worth the paper written on. Iran violated the provisions of that treaty by playing the same game used so effectively by North Korea. Iran strung the big six along by making promises and breaking them, providing assurances and cheating on them, permitting inspections and forbidding them, disclosing some locations and activities and hiding others. And the international community, led by the United States, forgave transgressions, extended deadlines, accepted excuses, and avoided imposing renewed sanctions. All this gave Iran ample time and opportunity to continue, overtly and covertly, to develop its nuclear program. Israel had been ready any number of times to slow the inevitable progress by bombing key Iranian facilities, but the United States had exerted enormous pressure to prevent that from being carried out.

Now the question is what will happen next? Will Iran provide the terror organizations it supports—Hezbollah in Lebanon, the Houthis in Yemen, and Hamas in Gaza—with even more dangerous weaponry than they already have? Will these radical political movements now have access to Iran's nuclear arsenal? Hezbollah (Party of God) is a long-time avowed enemy of Israel and the Houthis have a similar agenda. Their guiding slogan is "God is great, Death to America, Death to Israel, Curse on the Jews, Victory to Islam." Will Iran use these two terrorist outposts to strike at other countries in the Middle East? Or will Iran itself carry out its oft-heralded aim of "wiping Israel off the map" by attacking Israel with its newly acquired nuclear weapons? There is no question that, were that to occur, Israel would retaliate in kind. The resultant nuclear war would engulf the entire region, and could easily spread from there. The scenario is frightening to contemplate.

The New Caliphate

WORLD VIEW

By Harold Nelson

July 19, 2020

DUBAI, United Arab Emirates—Most of the modern nations in the Middle East are the artificial creations of the victorious allies of World War I. At the end of that war, the allies partitioned the defeated Ottoman Empire among themselves at the Paris Peace Conference (January 18, 1919 - January 16, 1920). Some thirty nations participated in the conference, but it was dominated by the Council of Four—Britain, France, the United States, and Italy. The conference established the League of Nations, which then awarded France mandates over Syria and Lebanon, and Britain mandates over Mesopotamia (later Iraq) and Palestine (later divided into Palestine and Transjordan). The redesigned Middle East has been a hot spot of trouble ever since, in part because the region was carved up with little regard to political, ethnic, and religious considerations of the people living there.

In recent years, the Middle East map has undergone change. Back in 2014, a group of radical Sunni fighters who had been battling Syria's strongman, Bashar al Assad, moved into Iraq. Calling themselves the Islamic State of Iraq and Syria (ISIS), they fought with the Iraqi army and the Kurds, and gained control over parts of Iraq. On July 29, 2014, the Shura (consultation) Council of ISIS declared the territory in both Syria and Iraq, which was under the control of ISIS, to constitute a Sunni Caliphate. At the time, the Caliphate stretched from Iraq's Diyala province, northeast of Baghdad, to Aleppo, in Syria's northwestern corner. Like all previous Caliphates, the ISIS Caliphate was a political-religious Muslim state, ruled by a Caliph, considered to be a successor to the prophet Muhammad. The appeal of the new Caliphate helped rally young radicalized Muslims who flocked to the area, eager to join ISIS in its fight. Hence, since establishment of the Caliphate, ISIS has continued to gain territory in both Syria and Iraq, and has done so with unfettered brutality and barbarism.

*

As of six years later, the map of the Middle East needs to be changed once again. Abdul Ahmed, the current Caliph, announced on July 9, 2020 that the Caliphate had made great strides toward eventual dominance of the Middle East. Specifically, he boasted that the Caliphate now controlled all of former Syria and almost all of former Iraq. In addition, the Caliphate had secured allegiance from three Sunni-controlled areas in non-contiguous territories.

Syria had fallen to ISIS after its recruits joined forces with the Syrian Free Army against their common enemy, the ruling Alawite minority. A concerted attack on both Damascus and Aleppo brought down the government of Bashar al Assad and saw much of the Alawite community massacred in the process. In Iraq, only two regions remained outside the Caliphate—a Kurdish-controlled northeastern corner and a Shia-controlled southern section. Kurdish Peshmerga forces had successfully defended their territory against ISIS attacks. Having staved these off, the Kurds declared independence and established their own state, Kurdistan, in the area. The densely-populated southern region in Iraq that had not been gobbled up by the Caliphate was the TE-Delta area, which had been run over and annexed by Iran in May of this year. Not wanting to provoke a direct confrontation with Iran, ISIS had left the TE-Delta untouched for the time being.

Except for these two areas, all of Iraq, including Baghdad, is now part of the ISIS Caliphate. The fall of Baghdad and its surroundings was engineered by Muqtada-al-Sadr, a firebrand Shia cleric who had been a powerful figure in the past but had withdrawn from politics in 2014. He reentered politics in the beginning of this year, at which time he reconstituted his Mahdi Army. Eager to be a key player in the mushrooming Caliphate,

Muqtada-al-Sadr joined forces with the Sunni ISIS. While a surprising move for a Shia cleric, his decision was not unprecedented since he had joined forces with Sunnis once before in 2013 to help oust then prime minister Nouri-al-Maliki. With Muqtada-al-Sadr on the side of ISIS, the fall of Baghdad was assured. Both the city and its environs were taken over with relatively few casualties. Soon thereafter, Muqtada-al-Sadr became an important voice of the Caliphate.

The three Sunni groups in non-contiguous territories that have declared their allegiance to the Caliphate are all terrorist organizations: Al Qaeda in Afghanistan (aided and abetted by the ruling Taliban), Al Qaeda in Yemen (known as AQAP or Al Qaeda in the Arabian Peninsula), and Boko Haram (literally, "Western Education is Forbidden") in Nigeria. AQAP has finally declared victory over the Houthis in Yemen after a protracted war. Thus, AQAP now controls the entire country of Yemen while the other two terrorist groups control significant portions of Afghanistan and Nigeria. This means that all three countries have large areas which can serve as safe havens and training grounds for ISIS. Inclusion of these areas in the Caliphate extends the latter's reach and enhances its power and prestige. All in all, radical Islamic terrorists can now operate out of four large land bases.

*

And what is life like in this Caliphate? So far, the Caliphate has been closed to all infidels. A few Muslim reporters have been allowed in, but their reports have been extensively censored. Most of what we know about the Caliphate comes from a number of individuals who have managed to escape and make it to the Free World. Their stories paint a picture of a brutal and barbaric state, worse than the one ruled over by the Taliban in Afghanistan. Thieves have their hands cut off. Women failing to wear the correct attire—armed clerics patrol the streets daily—are jailed. Strict Sharia law is observed throughout, and an extreme, ruthless form of Wahhabism is enforced. No religious variations are permitted. No religion other than that espoused by ISIS is tolerated. Anyone caught in some other religious observance is summarily shot on the spot. The same fate awaits apostates and anyone refusing to convert to the ISIS version of Islam. Gays and lesbians, if discovered, are hung at public squares. Female adulterers are stoned and male ones are buried alive, both types of executions are made into public spectacles. Anyone openly critical of the regime or attempting to oppose it is beheaded. Murderers and rapists are beheaded as well. All boys between the ages of 8 and 12 must attend a training session in beheading. And they must then carry out the brutal act on a doomed individual, taking the severed head home as a trophy. Any boy refusing to attend the training session is flogged in public until he either submits or dies.

This then is a thumbnail sketch of the Caliphate created by ISIS, the movement that the international community failed to destroy in its infancy. The Free World must do so now, before this cancer of the civilized world metastasizes any further.

The Growling Bear

WORLD VIEW

By Harold Nelson

April 3, 2022

KIEV, Ukraine—Last week's de facto annexation of all of Ukraine by Russia was slow in coming, but predictable considering the events that preceded it.

The first seminal event in this progression was Russia's annexation of Crimea in March 2014. Moscow claimed that Crimea had always been an integral part of Russia. While the move was strongly criticized as a gross violation of international law, little else was done to try and force Russia to reverse its unilateral action. Emboldened by the lack of a determined response, Russia then moved against Eastern Ukraine later that same year. It was clear that Russia was eager to secure a land bridge from its home territory to the newly acquired Crimea with its strategic outlet to the Black Sea. Eastern Ukraine was home to a large minority of ethnic Russians and these had begun to agitate for separation from Ukraine and for incorporation into Russia. The government of Ukraine tried to put down the simmering rebellion. In the ensuing struggle, the rebels were aided by Russia, which supplied them with arms. Before long, however, Russia intervened more directly by brazenly moving troops and armor across the border into Eastern Ukraine. This unprovoked military invasion of an independent country by another produced outrage in the West and led to the imposition of sanctions on Russia.

While the sanctions hurt the Russian economy, they were not drastic enough to stop the fighting that had erupted between Russian and Ukrainian forces. Ukraine appealed to the West for meaningful support, but the West refused to arm it to the extent necessary. A number of cease-fires between Russia and Ukraine were mediated by the United Nations and broken subsequently by one side or the other. The last such truce held until April 2018, but in May of that year Russia's foreign minister announced that his country was annexing Eastern Ukraine. In a press interview he stated that "Russia can no longer tolerate the harassment, discrimination, and hardship of its countrymen in Eastern Ukraine. Accordingly, the Kremlin has acceded to Eastern Ukraine's request to be separated from Ukraine and become a bona fide province of Russia."

*

The West did not react forcefully to Russia's annexation of Eastern Ukraine. The feeble response resembled that following Russia's earlier annexation of Crimea. Now as then, there were strong condemnations of the blatant violation of the territorial integrity of an independent nation. Other rhetorical statements denied Russia's claim that Eastern Ukraine's ethnic Russian minority was in such hardship, indeed danger, that it justified outside intervention. And the West threatened to impose additional sanctions. But no country was going to go to war with Russia over Eastern Ukraine. In fact, much as happened with Crimea, most western leaders seemed to regard the conflict as an internal problem involving Russia and one of its one-time provinces, a legacy left over from the disintegration of the former Soviet Union. Nor did Ukraine itself declare war on Russia over its lost eastern region. Ukraine knew that, by any realistic appraisal, it could not match Russia militarily. Quite the opposite. In a war, Russia could field a much larger number of soldiers, tanks, combat aircraft, and the like. Russia's military might would easily trump that of Ukraine.

The long struggle between Eastern Ukraine and Ukraine had hurt the economy of both. Eastern Ukraine had been the industrialized sector of the country, generating a quarter of Ukraine's GDP, a third of its exports, and providing essentially all of the coal Ukraine required. Now much of Eastern Ukraine's infrastructure was in shambles. Ukraine, on the other hand, had not suffered physical devastation but its treasury had been drained by the war, thereby endangering an economy that had already been teetering on the brink before the conflict started.

*

Two years passed since the annexation of Eastern Ukraine took effect. During that time, Russia poured large sums of money into Eastern Ukraine to shore up the local economy and restore the region to its earlier productivity. At the same time, Russia provided incentives which led substantial numbers of trained and educated Russians to settle in Eastern Ukraine. The result was that, by the end of 2020, Eastern Ukraine had made impressive advances in many areas and had recouped much of its erstwhile industrial strength.

Ukraine, by contrast, had continued to struggle financially and economically. It had appealed repeatedly to the World Bank, the International Monetary Fund, the United States and other western countries for massive aid, but the response had been tepid at best. Two years after having lost its eastern province, Ukraine was close to total economic collapse. Hopes of one day becoming a proud member of the European Union and of NATO had been dashed. People realized that there was no way that the country, in its current political and economic state, would be accepted into either of these organizations. Ukraine was left to fend on its own. When conditions failed to improve, people started to regard Eastern Ukraine with a measure of envy and longing. They began to take a second look at the path chosen by Eastern Ukraine. A new political party came into being in 2020. Calling itself "Slavic Brotherhood," the party advocated closer ties with Russia and ran pro-Russian candidates for political offices. As time went on, some politicians started to be outspoken about the desirability of Ukraine emulating the steps taken by its eastern province. Russia, at first covertly, but later on overtly, took an active part in these developments. Moscow played its hand adroitly through both its presence in Eastern Ukraine and its reliance on the ethnic Russian minority in Ukraine. It supported Slavic Brotherhood and stoked pro-Russian sentiments in the general population. It made the continuation of trade and loans contingent on the appointment of ethnic Russians to cabinet positions. Step-by-step, in a process eerily reminiscent of the "Anschluss" (joining, union)—Nazi Germany's annexation of Austria in 1938—Russia finagled the emergence of a pro-Russian government in Ukraine. When the issue was finally put to a vote in a national plebiscite held on March 28, 2022, an overwhelming majority voted for Ukraine to become a province of Mother Russia.

*

Now that Russia is firmly entrenched in Ukraine, fears are mounting as to what might come next. Will Russia be satisfied with its conquests or will it try and reach for more? With Ukraine having fallen, will the Baltic States be next? Census figures of 2020 showed that Estonia and Latvia had large ethnic Russian populations (about 30%) while Lithuania's was much smaller (about 6%). As distinct from Ukraine, the three Baltic States are members of NATO where countries (including the United States) are pledged to come to the defense of each other. Most analysts think it is unlikely that Russia would risk a military confrontation with the United States and, therefore, will forego outright military action against the Baltic States, at least for the time being. On the other hand, they warn about the likelihood of Russia employing yet again the strategy that has worked for it so well in Crimea, Eastern Ukraine, and Ukraine. Moscow, they believe, will try to undermine the Baltic democratic governments and institutions until these states will literally drop into Mother Russia's lap like ripe fruit falling off a tree. If that day comes, Moscow will have succeeded in re-asserting its full control over a sizable area of the defunct Soviet Union. It will be a day on which a new iron curtain will have descended over an important part of Europe. Quite possibly, it could also be the first day of a new cold war.

Piracy's Comeuppance

WORLD VIEW

By Michael Burns

August 21, 2022

BERBERA, Somalia—Somali piracy has plagued ships traversing the western part of the Indian Ocean since the end of the 20th century. The Indian Ocean is the world's third largest ocean, covering an area of over 26 million square miles, of which close to 3 million (about 2/3 of the area of the United States) have become afflicted by the scourge of piracy. Since some 80% of the world's shipping commerce moves through the Indian Ocean, Somali pirates have been provided with a wealth of targets.

The first piracy incident of modern times occurred on January 12, 1991, when bandits attacked and boarded the cargo ship *Naviluck*. Some of the crew were executed, and the ship was plundered and set on fire. Piracy incidents increased sharply during the first decade of the 21st century. In 2010, for example, there were 127 attacks and 26 ships were seized off the coast of Somalia. The pirates' heartland is Puntland, Somalia's northeastern region that encompasses the Horn of Africa. Puntland comprises about one third of Somalia's area and is home to one third of the country's population. Puntland's leaders declared it to be an autonomous state in 1998, but that has not been recognized internationally.

The pirates are Sunni Muslims and number an estimated 3,000 - 5,000. They operate out of four port cities in Puntland: Caluula, Eyl, Haradhere, and Hobyo. Pirates start out directly from a port or take off from a mother ship that is farther out to sea. Groups of 6 - 12 pirates, armed with machine guns and rocket-propelled grenades, use small skiffs to approach large ships, primarily freighters like tankers and container ships. Once at the target, they use grappling hooks, ladders, and ropes and attempt to attach those to the ship's first open (accessible) deck. This deck is relatively low above sea level for cargo ships, but much higher for cruise ships. Because of that, attacks on cruise ships have been rare. If successful in scaling the ship, the pirates proceed to subdue the crew. This is not difficult in the case of cargo ships because they carry small crews (as distinct from cruise ships) and because these crews are generally unarmed (most port authorities do not allow armed ships to enter their harbors). After subduing the crew, pirates move the ship and hostages to a Somali port and negotiate for ransom. Over the years, insurance companies have paid out hundreds of millions of dollars in ransom and other costs.

*

Many measures have been taken to deter piracy in the Indian Ocean. Ships have installed LRADs (long range acoustic devices) that transmit powerful and pain-inducing sounds to disorient approaching pirates. Other instruments emit high energy light beams designed to blind pirates' vision. Open decks have been surrounded with razor wire or electrified fences, and equipped with water hoses and powerful water jets to be aimed at approaching boats. Shipping companies have hired private security guards and converted a few old small ships to floating armories from which arms can be dispatched by speedboats to threatened ships. And four multinational naval coalitions patrol the Indian Ocean area at risk. Combined Task Force 150 (CTF-150), built around the U.S. 5th fleet, was set up after September 11, 2001 for counter-terrorism activity, but was subsequently assigned anti-piracy duties as well. In 2008, the European Union launched its naval force (EU NAVFOR), and NATO provided a 7-warship flotilla. Lastly, in 2009, Combined Task Force 151 (CTF-151) was set up, which took over the anti-piracy duties from CTF-150.

*

But all of these measures have failed to eradicate Somali piracy. While incidents decreased for a while after 2018, they increased again significantly beginning in 2021. The trigger for this was the fall of Yemen's government to the Houthis in 2015. This upheaval worked against Al Qaeda in the Arabian Peninsula (AQAP, a Sunni group and long the most dangerous and powerful offshoot of the original Al Qaeda), which was trying to take full control of Yemen. In August 2020, AQAP went on the offensive, succeeded in ousting the Shia Houthis, and took over the entire country. Thus in Yemen, a mere stone's throw away from Somalia across the Gulf of Aden, a Sunni government friendly to the Sunni pirates had come to power. While piracy had not been the stock-in-trade of AQAP, the group's leadership realized that piracy was yet another way of striking at the West. Therefore it made sense for AQAP to provide the pirates with as much support as possible, especially since such cooperation could be made lucrative for AQAP. With these thoughts in mind, AQAP contacted the pirates and offered to supply them with boats, arms, other equipment, and actionable intelligence on international shipping and on the measures taken to protect this shipping. In return, AQAP exacted an agreement on profit-sharing of the ransoms the pirates would collect. With such backing it was not surprising that, beginning in 2021, piracy increased again.

*

The first three months of 2022 brought on numerous attacks on major shipping lines (Maersk, MSC, Hapag-Lloyd, NYK, and others). A significant number were successful. More crews were taken hostage than ever before and huge sums of ransom were paid out. It was enough to finally rouse the West to undertake decisive offensive action to bring the scourge to an end, once and for all. On August 3, 2022 a multinational attack on Somali piracy was initiated. NATO countries cooperated with the United States, China, Japan, and India in mounting a coordinated land, sea, and air operation. Planes were launched from aircraft carriers in the Indian Ocean and from land bases in Kenya and Saudi Arabia. The planes pounded and strafed harbors and port facilities in Caluula, Eyl, Haradhere, and Hobyo, the cities that had served as the pirates' safe havens. Warships stationed off the coast added their fire to the aerial bombardment. In a short time, harbors and water fronts were leveled and vessels of all sizes at anchor in the harbors were destroyed.

Once the air and sea bombardment had been completed, helicopters dropped special operations forces who spread throughout the cities, targeting pirates' hideouts. Many pirates and key pirate leaders were killed; others were arrested and jailed. Extensive surveillance had succeeded in locating three mother ships used by the pirates. Those were destroyed with Tomahawk missiles.

At the conclusion of the operation, a command center was set up at the port city of Berbera in Somaliland, the region northwest of Puntland. Somaliland was formerly a British colony, but is now an autonomous region of Somalia. The northern coastline of Somaliland constitutes the southern border of the Gulf of Aden. Berbera is close to the western end of the gulf and the entrance to the Red Sea. The intention was to have a powerful coast guard, other navy vessels, helicopters, and special operations forces operate out of Berbera, conduct routine patrols of Puntland's coastline and take action as needed. At the same time, an international effort would be made to bring stability to all of Somalia by working to improve the governance, education, and economy of the country. Hopefully, these steps will prevent a resurgence of Somali piracy and will end this chapter of a modern-day scourge.

The Spread of Terror

WORLD VIEW

By Harold Nelson

June 25, 2023

ABUJA, Nigeria—Nigeria is Africa's most populous nation (164 million in 2011). It became a British Protectorate in 1901 and gained full independence in 1960. Since then it has had a tumultuous political history, replete with military rulers, coups, ethnic and religious clashes. In 2002 it saw the birth of Boko Haram (literally, "Western Education is Forbidden"), a militant Islamic group intent on overthrowing the Nigerian government and establishing an Islamic state. The group was founded in Maiduguri, capital of the Nigerian state of Borno, in Nigeria's northeastern corner. The group has grown to become an extremely violent terrorist organization that has caused mayhem in Nigeria through waves of bombings (including suicide bombings), assassinations, burning of villages, massacres, and kidnappings. It has been estimated that by the end of 2014 Boko Haram had killed over 11,000 people, kidnapped over 500 (including 276 schoolgirls), and caused close to two million people to flee the conflict zone.

Boko Haram is a fundamentalist and puritanical group, believed to have perhaps 10,000 members, many of whom follow Salafism doctrines. The group promotes a version of Islam that forbids Muslims to take part in any political or social activity associated with western society, including such things as voting in elections, wearing shirts and trousers, or receiving a secular education. Interestingly though, like other Islamic terrorist groups intent on turning the political clock back hundreds of years, they have no problem embracing other products of modernity such as cell phones and other electronic equipment, pick-up trucks equipped with machine guns, and all manner of arms, ammunition, bombs and explosives.

*

In the spring of this year, Boko Haram captured Maiduguri, and shortly thereafter consolidated its hold on the entire state of Borno, which it declared to be part of the ISIS Caliphate. Two weeks ago the terrorist organization moved another step closer to its ultimate goal of asserting its control over all of Nigeria. The group mounted two simultaneous attacks on Damaturu, capital of the state of Yobe, and on Yola, capital of the state of Adamawa. Both cities fell after three days of vicious fighting, whereupon Boko Haram consolidated its hold on the remaining areas of the two states. Once that had been accomplished, the group declared Yobe and Adamawa to be part of the Caliphate, much as it had done for Borno. With that, Boko Haram had taken full control of three of Nigeria's thirty-six states.

Roughly speaking, Yobe and Adamawa lie to the west and south of Borno, respectively. These three states make up Nigeria's northeastern corner and as such share borders with three adjacent African nations: Niger, Chad, and Cameroon. In the past, Boko Haram had already conducted raids into these adjacent countries. Now that it controls greatly extended sections of these shared borders, Boko Haram's raids into Niger, Chad, and Cameroon are bound to increase in both frequency and intensity. There is little doubt that such "neighborly" intervention will have a pronounced destabilizing effect on those countries.

With Boko Haram controlling three Nigerian states, the Caliphate has been greatly expanded. Even though these states are not contiguous with Iraq, the two strongholds are actively communicating with each other. What is not clear at the moment is whether Boko Haram will push to get more of Nigeria's thirty-six states under its control, or whether it will put its efforts into carving out sections from Niger, Chad, and Cameroon instead. Either way, Boko Haram is bound to exacerbate the instability in that part of Africa and to spread the reign of terror over an ever increasing area.

The Caliphate Grows

WORLD VIEW

By Harold Nelson

October 8, 2023

RABAT, Morocco—Africa, the continent believed to be the birthplace of humanity, has had a long and eventful history. Africa has largely been spared some types of natural disasters such as floods, tornadoes, hurricanes, earthquakes, and volcanic eruptions, though it has had its share of famines, droughts, and diseases. On the other hand, Africa has definitely experienced a plethora of man-made disasters. Modern times have brought colonialism, slave trade, apartheid, dictatorships, and genocide. During the era of colonialism, Africa had been exploited by European countries who literally mined the continent for its riches. With few exceptions, the colonial powers did not prepare the native populations for eventual independence. Hence, once the colonial era came to an end and the African countries became independent, they were not prepared to take on the mantle of responsible self government. The result has been never-ending wars between tribes and factions, rampant official corruption, pervasive poverty, and brutal tyrants that have caused much of the continent to lag behind the rest of the world. Libya is a prime example of this state of affairs.

Colonel Muammar Gaddafi seized power in Libya from King Idris in 1969. He ruled Libya with an iron hand, incredible brutality, and complete repression of freedom of expression, political debate, and all other aspects of a civil society. The tyranny lasted for 42 years until Gaddafi's overthrow in 2011. The end came when he was dragged, wounded and bleeding, from a storm drain where he had been hiding, and then shot. Ever since, Libya has been plagued by violence, instability, and lawlessness. The country's elections have yielded a succession of failed governments, thereby increasing the danger of promoting instability in neighboring African countries.

The basic reason for Libya's internal turmoil lies in the existence of a large number of separate militias, well over 1,500, each controlling a specific territory. The militias are concentrated in Libya's northern fertile strip, home to the bulk of Libya's population (estimated at about 6 million in 2014). The strip borders the Mediterranean Sea and has a coastline of 1,100 miles, the longest of any African country bordering the Mediterranean. The strip makes up about a third of the country's land area, the rest being part of the Sahara desert.

The militias were united in their hatred of Gaddafi and in their determination to overthrow him, but beyond that they had little in common. They were, and still are, split along many different lines—Islamic, secessionist, liberal, ethnic, regional, local. What makes matters worse is that the militias are now awash in weapons looted from Gaddafi's arsenals. And having lived for over four decades under a dictatorship, they have no grounding in government and no understanding of democracy. They are not versed in the art of compromise and the rule of law. Each militia is out for its own share of money, power, arms, and territory.

*

At the start of this year, the political landscape of Libya's northern strip could only be described as a hodgepodge of governing entities. The internationally recognized government of the country had fled the onslaught of the militias and was now quartered in the port city of Tobruk, the easternmost city of the strip, close to the border with Egypt. Going westward from there along the strip were six militias that controlled the following cities: (1) Derna, said to be the most pious city in Libya and one that has a long record of radicalism. (2) Ben Ghazi, Libya's second largest city and site of the 2012 attack on the U.S. embassy. Ben Ghazi is controlled by an Islamist radical militia, said to be the most heavily armed and most dangerous of Libya's militias. (3) Brega, a port city with an important oil refinery and oil export facilities. (4) Sirte, the birthplace of Gaddafi and site of many governmental departments during the Gaddafi era. (5) Misrata, Libya's third largest city, sometimes called the business capital of Libya. (6) Tripoli, Libya's capital and largest city. Tripoli is a port city and commercial and manufacturing center located at the western end of the strip, close to the border with Tunisia. The militias of Derna, Brega, Sirte, and Misrata are affiliated with the Islamic State of Iraq and Syria (ISIS) and have declared the areas under their control to be part of the ISIS Caliphate.

*

A major development occurred in July of this year when three battle-hardened jihadists from ISIS arrived in Libya. They had been dispatched to persuade leaders of the militias controlling Ben Ghazi and Tripoli to follow the other coastal militias' lead by affiliating with ISIS and declaring their territories to be part of the ISIS Caliphate. In return, ISIS offered the militias financial and military support to help them plan and execute a multi-militia, all-out assault on Tobruk with the goal of ousting the internationally recognized Libyan government. It was a deal the two militias were loathe to reject. And so, on August 15, 2023, the Ben Ghazi and Tripoli militias declared their allegiance to ISIS and designated the territories under their control as belonging to the Caliphate.

During the following weeks, all six militias made preparations for an attack on Tobruk. There was heavy traffic of both men and materiel all along Libya's coastal strip. Fighters and armaments were assembled in both Derna and Ben Ghazi. Since the militias already controlled most of the strip, all preparations for the attack were made openly. While that was going on, civilians fled Tobruk en masse and sought shelter in neighboring Egypt. The government in Tobruk, aware of the impending attack, appealed to the international community for immediate help, but no nation was keen on entering the Libyan quagmire for a second time after the bloody uprising of 2011. The actual assault on Tobruk came on September 26, 2023. As expected, the government forces were no match for the combined might of the six militias. Tobruk fell after three days and with that, the entire coastal strip became an integral part of the ISIS Caliphate. Since this strip is home to the majority of Libya's population, the net effect is that, for all practical purposes, all of Libya has now become part of the Caliphate. Hence, a new and large base has been created for radical Islamic terrorists to be used freely for training purposes and for planning future operations. Moreover, the terrorists now have easy access to southern Europe via the Mediterranean. Carnage is waiting at Europe's doorstep.

Enough is Enough

WORLD VIEW

By Michael Burns

August 4, 2024

TEL AVIV, Israel—The eastern part of the Mediterranean Sea is flanked by the *Fertile Crescent*, a roughly semicircular land mass which begins at the northern end of the Persian Gulf, stretches from there through Iran, Iraq, Syria, Lebanon, Israel, Jordan, and Egypt where it ends up at the southern end of the Nile Valley. The crescent is called fertile because it is thought to have had a more moderate, agriculturally productive climate in the past than it does today. The central part of this region, the narrow strip of land on both sides of the Jordan River that makes up the modern states of Israel and Jordan, has been conquered and liberated by a seemingly endless progression of powers that have swept across it from the north or the south. In recent times, it has been the battle ground for the Israeli-Palestinian conflict.

That conflict had the distinction of getting close to becoming another of the world's Hundred Years' Wars, having already lasted 76 years, from 1948 to 2024. It appears, however, that Israel's Artzeinu Tamid party may have now brought the conflict to an abrupt halt by offering a radical new agenda. Of course, it remains to be seen whether the halt will prove to be only temporary or whether it will lead to a permanent resolution of the conflict. Here is what transpired. In the election held on July 17, 2024, Artzeinu Tamid ("our land always" in Hebrew) garnered a stunning 65 of the 120 seats in the Knesset (parliament). In the past, Israeli governments usually had to operate by forging a number of more or less willing parties into a working coalition. Not so after this election. Since Artzeinu Tamid now commands a majority in the Knesset, it can govern without being beholden to any other party, and can put its proposed drastic new approach to the Israeli-Palestinian conflict into effect.

Artzeinu Tamid grew out of the National Religious Party, founded in 1956, and the Habayit Hayehudi Party ("the Jewish home" in Hebrew), founded in 2008. The platforms of these two parties had catered to the religious segment of Israel's population. In 2020, Artzeinu Tamid decided to make the party more appealing to a wider segment of the country's population. The party's leadership made some compromises on religious issues that the party's religious base could still live with but that made the party more attractive to the non-religious. (In 2020, Israelis categorized themselves as 8% ultra-orthodox, 12% religious, 13% traditional, 25% not very religious, and 42% secular). At the same time, the party advanced a platform the centerpiece of which was a radically new approach to the age-old Israeli-

Palestinian conflict. The result was that Israelis flocked to Artzeinu Tamid in droves and party membership grew by leaps and bounds. People saw a light at the end of a long tunnel and wanted to be part of the effort that might finally deliver peace and security.

*

Uri Ben-Ami, Artzeinu Tamid's charismatic leader, was interviewed on July 19, 2024, by Mike Sorenson of CNN. First, he summarized the current situation. "Most Israelis," Ben-Ami said, "no longer care about trying to solve the Israeli-Palestinian conflict because they know that it is unsolvable—at least for the next one hundred years. The two state solution is a mirage. The Palestinians could have had their state several times over, beginning with the partition of Palestine in 1947. They rejected that and countless Israeli offers made since. Land for peace hasn't worked either. Israel withdrew from the Gaza Strip, leaving behind useful infrastructure. The Arabs could have made Gaza into a Middle Eastern Singapore. Instead, they elected Hamas, a terrorist organization, to govern, demolished the Israeli-made infrastructure, set up rocket launchers in civilian enclaves, promoted a culture of death, and completely ruined the strip's economy. Both there and in the West Bank, Palestinians continue to indoctrinate their youth with hatred for Israel and Jews and the glory of suicide bombers. In short, they are doing everything except sitting down to negotiate a peaceful settlement. And all the time rocket barrages, suicide attacks, kidnappings, and a variety of other hostile acts go on unabated. Can you blame the Israelis for finally having had enough of all of this?" Then he quoted key portions of the party's platform:

> We declare that the State of Israel extends from the current border with Jordan to the Mediterranean and from the current border with Lebanon to the current border with Egypt, but excludes the Gaza Strip and the current Palestinian-controlled area of the West Bank.
>
> We declare that no Palestinian state shall be created on any part of the State of Israel.
>
> We confirm that Jerusalem is the capital of the State of Israel and that it shall never be divided.
>
> We advocate the unilateral annexation by Israel of the Golan Heights currently under Israeli control. The people living there now are entitled to have their "no man's land" status terminated by incorporating the territory unambiguously into Israel.
>
> We advocate the unilateral annexation by Israel of the West Bank area that currently contains all of the Jewish settlements. Palestinians living in this area can either be-

come Israeli citizens or move to the Palestinian-controlled area of the West Bank.

We propose that the Palestinian-controlled area of the West Bank be administered as its residents see fit: the area can retain its current status, become an independent entity (singly or jointly with the Gaza Strip), or opt for annexation by Jordan.

We propose that the Gaza Strip be administered as its residents see fit: the area can retain its current status, become an independent entity (singly or jointly with the West Bank), or opt for annexation by Egypt.

We state clearly and unequivocally that, in the event of a violent or hostile act against Israel (rockets, raids across the border, suicide attacks, kidnappings, etc.) from either the Gaza Strip or the West Bank, and committed by Hamas, the Palestinian authority, or some other entity, Israel shall consider this an *act of war* and will respond accordingly. Israel will immediately cut off all water, electricity and other supplies (including financial funds) that it provides the area from which the attack originated. Israel will also immediately revoke all permits issued to residents of that area that allow them entry into Israel for work. These measures shall remain in effect until the perpetrators of the hostile act have been brought to justice by the pertinent Palestinian authority. Failure to do so promptly and to the fullest extent may result in Israeli military incursion with the possible annexation of territory and expulsion of its Arab population.

Mike Sorenson then asked Ben-Ami whether his party would be ready to face the condemnation by the international community that was sure to follow. "They have been condemning us for years," Ben-Ami replied, "while we bent over backwards and gave and gave and gave without ever getting anything in return. So let them continue to condemn us. What else is new?"

Time will tell if there will be a new dawn in the Middle East or just more war.

The Dragon Stirs

WORLD VIEW

By James Morrison

September 15, 2024

MACAU, China—Macau is a popular tourist destination for visitors to the Orient. Located just 40 miles west of Hong Kong in China's Pearl River delta, it is easily reached by plane or boat. Macau comprises a city and two small islands. The city lies on the Macau Peninsula and the islands, Taipa and Coloane, are connected to the mainland via bridges and reclaimed land. Macau had been under Portuguese rule since 1557, but on December 19, 1999 reverted to China in accordance with a joint Sino-Portuguese declaration signed in 1987. The latter stipulated that China was to treat Macau as a Special Administrative Region (SAR), thereby granting Macau's citizens considerable independence. The Chinese government guaranteed that it would not interfere with Macau's way of life and capitalist system for at least 50 years because China accepted a principle of "one country, two systems." Hence, for some twenty-five years, Macau has enjoyed a privileged environment compared to the rest of China. Its residents have been able to live their lives in an atmosphere of freedom and to conduct their business affairs under a capitalist umbrella.

All this changed abruptly five days ago. On September 10, 2024, the government of the People's Republic of China (PRC) sent a directive to Min Wang, Chief Executive and Administrator of Macau, informing him that the PRC was revoking Macau's SAR status, effective immediately. "Times have changed," the directive explained, "and what was appropriate and acceptable in 1999 no longer holds today. Specifically, the tax revenue sharing plan adopted in 1999 no longer functions as intended. China's income from Macau has steadily decreased, but China's expenditures for the region have risen continuously. Maintaining the SAR status for Macau has become an unsustainable financial burden for the PRC. Hence, the need for a political readjustment." The reason for China's declining revenue from Macau is an open secret. Nowadays, easily accessible casinos can be found on every continent. No one needs to travel any longer half-way around the world to gamble in Macau. As a result, Macau's casinos have seen a sharp drop in attendance. The concomitant decrease in casino profits has led to smaller tax payments to the mainland. And there is no indication conditions will change in the foreseeable future.

*

The reaction in Macau to the PRC directive was muted. Only one protest was organized in response. Some six hundred people gathered at the Macau Tower. There were a few brief speeches exhorting the protesters to vent their grievances to the authorities. Following the speakers, the crowd began to move toward the Macau Government Headquarters. They marched along Avenida Dr. Stanley Ho (named after Stanley Ho, billionaire and casino owner) and Avenida da Praia Grande, and finally assembled in front of the impressive government offices' building which had served as the Governor's Palace prior to 1999. Once there, the crowd requested a meeting with Min Wang. After some back and forth, a delegation of protesters was admitted into the building and met with the Chief Executive. They asked for retraction of the directive, or at least for extension of Macau's SAR status, but Wang told them that he was powerless to do anything regarding PRC's new policy. Unhappy, but probably not surprised, the protesters left and dispersed. There was no violence. Grudgingly, Macau's residents reconciled themselves to living under the new system of jurisdiction.

A senior official who spoke to us on condition of anonymity explained the lack of a strong response as follows: "First of all," he said, "allowing Min Wang to continue as Macau's administrator was a smart move by the PRC because it avoided a government shake-up. Though Wang was not all that liked, retaining him did provide continuity and helped calm tempers. But even more importantly, Beijing had prepared the ground for years by targeting government employees, teachers, businessmen and other leaders of the community who professed a pan-China view." When asked what he meant by having people targeted, he elaborated. "These people were assiduously cultivated, bribed, promoted, perhaps even blackmailed, to become more outspoken about abolishing Macau's SAR status and more proactive in recruiting others to this point of view. A prime example of this strategy was the mainland's fostering close ties with Min Wang and the two Chief Executives who preceded him. As a result, these individuals expressed their wish to see the SAR status revoked, and did so publicly and frequently. 'We need to be like the rest of the country,' they would say and, acting on their conviction, proceeded to appoint departmental secretaries and other officials who were like-minded."

Internationally, the reaction to China's move was also limited. Perhaps other countries, much as the PRC itself, considered this strictly a Chinese internal affair. Moreover, at this juncture in time, Macau had ceased to be a significant trade center or a valuable military outpost. Whatever events transpired there were judged to have minor impact on surrounding countries and even less on the world at large. The White House issued a statement deploring the sudden unilateral abrogation of China's contractual obligation under the terms of the 1999 Sino-Portuguese declaration. The European Union, NATO (North Atlantic Treaty

Organization), and SEATO (Southeast Asia Treaty Organization) expressed their dismay with this political change, but did not go further. And all resolutions introduced by the United States and others in the United Nations Security Council were dead on arrival. China, a permanent member of the Council, vetoed all immediately.

Only Hong Kong, undoubtedly fearful of being next and losing its own SAR status, raised a red flag. The *Hong Kong Daily Sun* warned that acquiescence by the world community to any violation of international agreements by a country (in this case, China) merely served to embolden that country to ignore other international obligations and/or commit even worse offenses. "That's the way it has always been," the paper said. "One example suffices. Lack of a forceful response to Hitler's remilitarization of the Rhineland in 1936, in violation of the 1919 Treaty of Versailles, led to further Nazi aggression and ultimately to World War II. Clearly, democratic governments ignore violations of international treaties at their peril. As George Santayana had admonished many years ago, '*Those who cannot learn from history are doomed to repeat it.*"

*

Loss of its SAR status is a sad milestone in Macau's history. The Ming Court leased Macau to Portugal in 1557, thereby making Macau the first European colony in East Asia. Macau evolved into a hub for trade routes and an outpost of Western religions. It flourished over 200 years until the Dutch and the British began to control the trading routes in East Asia in the 1800s. In 1849 Portugal claimed sovereignty over Macau and this was recognized by China in 1887. In the 1960s, legal gambling was introduced and Macau became known as the "Las Vegas of Asia." It was the only place in China where gambling was legal. In the 1960s and 1970s Macau gained notoriety as a Mecca for prostitution and crime. Then came the joint Sino-Portuguese declaration of 1987 according to which Macau was to revert to China in 1999 and receive SAR status. That transition took place as planned, and Macau has prospered since until the fateful day of September 10, 2024.

Now that Macau has been absorbed by mainland China, it is bound to lose its freewheeling character and, sooner or later, many vestiges of some 450 years of Portuguese colonial heritage.

Tahrir Square Reprise

WORLD VIEW

By Harold Nelson

March 7, 2027

CAIRO, Egypt—The Muslim Brotherhood was founded in 1928 in Egypt by Hassan al-Banna, an ardent admirer of Adolf Hitler and the Nazi regime. The Brotherhood was founded as an Islamist, religious, and political movement. Though many claim that the Brotherhood decries violence, the organization is often viewed as the root source of Islamic terrorism and remains committed to militancy. Its members have included Abdullah Azzam (Osama bin Laden's mentor), Ayman al-Zawahiri (Al Qaeda's leader after Osama bin Laden), and Khalid Sheikh Mohammed (mastermind of the 9/11 attack). The Brotherhood has branches in some 70 countries and territories and claims to have taken part in most pro-Islamic conflicts from the Arab-Israeli war of 1948 to the Arab Spring of 2011. The group's ideology has had a profound influence on the terrorist organizations of Hamas and Hezbollah. The Brotherhood was part of the anti-communist opposition in the Soviet-Afghan war, and it is alleged to be a key factor in the ongoing Chechen revolt.

The Brotherhood advocates a return to the precepts of the Koran. It rejects Western influences and sanctions *Jihad* and *Fatwas*. The organization's motto is "Allah is our objective. The Prophet is our leader. Koran is our law. Jihad is our way. Dying in the way of Allah is our highest hope." Under President Hosni Mubarak, who ruled Egypt from 1981 to 2011, the Egyptian Brotherhood was relatively inactive. Because of fierce oppression by Mubarak, it limited itself to functioning primarily as a social organization. It kept its political and military wings largely underground. This changed after the revolution of 2011 when the Brotherhood emerged empowered, garnered 36% of the vote, and saw its candidate, Mohamed Morsi, win the presidency. At that time, the Brotherhood also gained renewed prominence in other countries, such as Tunisia, Morocco, and Jordan. Morsi was ousted by General Abdel-Fatah al-Sisi in 2013 and since then Egypt has been ruled once again by a series of military dictatorships.

The current president, General Ali Hasani, has followed in his predecessors' footsteps and clamped down tightly on the Brotherhood. Many of the organization's activists have been jailed (several have been executed) and the remaining ones are under constant surveillance. As a result, the Brotherhood has once again limited itself to social activism and has kept its political and military wings securely under cover. The general population has not fared much better because, here too, Hasani has continued the governance that preceded him. He has suppressed dissent, banned opposition parties, taken political prisoners, conducted sham trials, and given the police and the hated Central Security free reign. Egypt has descended into another Mubarak-type tyranny. Fear, anger, and discontent are widespread. People have become restive and anxious to rid the country of Hasani.

*

That was when the Brotherhood seized the opportunity. It all started about three weeks ago when Facebook and other social media began to carry messages from the Brotherhood. "Let us throw off the yoke of dictatorship," the communications urged. "Let us work together. We erred in not joining the protest early in 2011. We will not repeat that error. We stand ready to lead the protest now." The statement went on to say that the Brotherhood would no longer let itself be tyrannized by the country's military dictatorships. And it called for all, regardless of their religious or secular persuasion, to join forces. They stated their own position clearly. "We no longer accept being excluded from the political arena. We are an integral part of Egypt and demand to be treated as such. We call on all like-minded Egyptians to join us in a protest rally at Tahrir Square on Friday, February 26, 2027. Long live a free Egypt." Stacks of pamphlets, carrying the same message, were left overnight at key intersections in Cairo.

Fear and anger had become so widespread that people were ready to take their chances with anyone promising to bring relief, including the Muslim Brotherhood. Many people welcomed the Brotherhood's leadership in this effort and for two good reasons. First, the Brotherhood was well-known for its legendary grassroots machinery. With that aid in place, the protest movement stood a good chance of rousing a large number of protesters required for success. Second, people felt that since the Brotherhood constituted a significant part of the country's population, it should be included in the political process.

On Friday, February 26, 2027, the protest rally took place as planned. A sizable crowd gathered at Tahrir Square. At first, the authorities adopted a wait and see approach. They allowed two speakers to address the gathering. After that they demanded that the crowd clear the square. When people refused to withdraw, the authorities opened up with water cannons and tear gas to disperse the crowd. Four hours after the gathering, the square had returned to its traditional quiet state. The Brotherhood has now called for a second, large protest demonstration to be held this coming Friday, March 12, 2027, at Tahrir Square, and designated it (as in 2011) a "Day of Rage."

Now the big question is, what comes next? Will this turn into a second Arab Spring? And if it does, what will the outcome be?

A Rude Awakening

WORLD VIEW

By Harold Nelson

March 18, 2029

BRUSSELS, Belgium—On March 5, 2029, Peter Olsen, the current Danish director of the European Union's Secretariat-General, called a special meeting. The Secretariat-General is one of forty Directorates-General that together constitute the European Commission. The latter, in turn, is one of seven key organizations that manage the European Union—the umbrella organization of twenty-eight European nations. The Secretariat-General is one of the central services of the European Commission, facilitating its smooth and effective functioning and providing strategic direction.

For the March meeting, the Secretariat-General met at their regular venue on the 13th floor of the Berlaymont building in downtown Brussels. Olsen came right to the point. "I've called this special meeting," he began, "so that we can discuss a recent disturbing development that, I feel, requires a concerted response by the European Union. Since the Secretariat-General is charged with defining the European Commission's strategic objectives and priorities, I feel that it is entirely appropriate for us to be discussing this issue here and now."

With that he explained that the development which concerned him deeply was the accelerated rise of extremism throughout Europe. There were two faces to this extremism. On the one hand, there was the resurgence of neo-Nazi and other far-right groups. On the other hand, there was the growth of radicalized elements within the Muslim communities. "Let me take the first face first," Olsen said. "I am sure you are aware that gains of political strength by neo-Nazi and related groups have been particularly pronounced in Hungary, Belgium, and Greece, not to mention the previous fascist strongholds of Germany, Austria, and Italy. In all six of these countries, membership in far-right parties has grown considerably, thereby granting those parties newfound political clout. Quite a few of their candidates have been elected to parliament so that they can broadcast their strident rhetoric readily from a public forum. Moreover, in practically every European country there has been a rise of hate-driven acts, both violent and non-violent, committed by far-right extremists and targeting primarily Jewish communities and secondarily our large Muslim immigrant communities."

As to the causes fueling the rise of right-wing extremism, Olsen enumerated several: political instability of some countries where governments have fallen and elections are said to have been fraudulent; a level of anxiety across the continent because of a general lack of military preparedness; economic woes of some countries which have resulted in galloping inflation and large-scale unemployment; Europe's impotence in countering recent Russian aggression. "And of course," he added, "let's not forget the latent and not so latent, two thousand year-old despicable and irrational hatred of Jews—the convenient scapegoat that individuals and societies blame for their own shortcomings and problems."

The perils of rising far-right extremism, as Olsen saw it, were twofold. "First, as extremism acquires political power it is likely to mount attacks on civil liberties, a first step on the road to dictatorships. We have been there before and we must do everything we can to prevent us from going there again. Second, empowered extremism leads to brain drain. Countries will lose valuable people as top scientists, doctors, researchers, and creative artists head for the exits. This will certainly apply to our Jewish minorities, but to other groups as well." And significant brain drain, he stressed, was bound to have a negative effect on the economy and thereby inevitably enhance the appeal of right-wing extremism even further. Hence, Olsen felt, there was an urgent need for a concerted educational effort to enlighten Europe's population about the dangers of granting legitimacy and power to extremist parties by contributing to them, joining them, or voting for them. Summing up, he said, "People must understand that such actions are tantamount to playing with fire."

*

Then Olsen proceeded to discuss the other face of extremism, namely the growth of radicalized Islamists. He began by mentioning two well-known characteristics of Europe's Muslim communities. One was the higher birth rate of these communities compared to those of other groups. This meant that the proportion of Muslims in the general population was steadily increasing leading some to warn that Europe was on a path to becoming Eurabia. Whether true or not, being slowly outnumbered in their own country by what many consider to be foreigners and intruders engenders a great deal of fear and resentment in the native population, thereby aiding neo-Nazis and the like in recruiting new converts to their ranks.

The second characteristic of Muslim communities was that, by and large, and for a number of reasons, their members have not assimilated well into local cultures. Because of that, Muslims feel largely disenfranchised and frequently lack the identification with, and loyalty to, their adopted country. Though they immigrated to Europe primarily to raise their quality of life many have failed to find suitable employment, especially younger immigrants. The resultant large numbers of unemployed youths are disenchanted and see few prospects for the future. They become easy prey for agitators and recruiters for violence. A significant number of young Muslims end up as Islamic radicals, venting their rage and frustration through violence against the state or, more frequently, against the Jews. Olsen pointed out that most of the immigrant Muslims hailed from the Middle East, a region where they had been indoctrinated from the cradle on with virulent anti-Semitism (often cloaked as hatred of Israel), in their homes, schools, and mosques. Having exported their hatred to Europe, it has become an integral part of Europe's anti-Semitic scene. "Thus," Olsen said, "Europe is now host to two groups of extremists, neo-Nazis and Islamic radicals, who are united in their hatred of Jews and Israel. Both groups engage in spreading anti-Semitic propaganda, defiling synagogues and cemeteries, and committing physical attacks on Jews, including outright killings."

*

It was ironic, according to Olsen, that despite the unemployment situation, Muslims were still immigrating to Europe, still hoping to improve their quality of life. However, once they arrive, employment and assimilation problems of these enlarged Muslim communities are only exacerbated. "Hence," he said, "I believe that we should discuss whether or not to recommend that Europe institute a quota system or at least some kind of unified immigration policy for Muslims."

He then mentioned two other problems emanating from Muslim communities. One was that a growing number of Muslims, all across Europe, were using Shariah law to settle their disputes. The mushrooming of Shariah-based tribunals, mediation, counseling, and dispute resolution centers was leading to establishment of two parallel legal systems. This, he felt, was extremely troubling because establishing a legal duality would undermine the state's authority and may bring on political instability. In the long run, the result would likely be an infringement on civil liberties, especially since Shariah law was much more restrictive than Western democratic law. "We must develop suitable guidelines for dealing with this issue," Olsen said.

Finally, he described another worrisome development. A new strategy had taken root in some Muslim communities. Fearful of being targets for neo-Nazis and other extremists, and having lost confidence in the government's resolve to protect them, Muslims decided to take matters into their own hands. Several communities, especially sizable ones, have organized their own security contingents that patrol the streets on a routine basis. Teams of 2-5 people roam Muslim neighborhoods, armed only with clubs, cell phones, and walkie-talkies. While the action is certainly understandable, there is growing concern about these security patrols hampering police action or worse yet, planting the seeds for creation of actual Muslim militias down the road.

"This is my take," Olsen concluded. "Now let me open the floor for discussion. My hope is that ultimately we can come to a consensus and formulate recommendations for pro-active measures to deal with the issues I have outlined. These recommendations would then be submitted to the European Commission for consideration. Obviously, we won't be able to do all this in one short meeting. Therefore, I will schedule as many additional ones as needed."

A lively and lengthy discussion followed Olsen's presentation. Future meetings were then scheduled. It remains to be seen what recommendations the Secretariat-General arrives at.

The Dragon Strikes

WORLD VIEW

By James Morrison

July 15, 2029

HONG KONG, China—Fabled Hong Kong, often called the Pearl of the Orient, is a vibrant metropolis that lies on China's eastern coast, at the Pearl River delta. The area consists today of Hong Kong Island, the Kowloon peninsula, and the New Territories. The latter comprise a large land area north of Kowloon as well as more than 250 outlying islands. Hong Kong is densely populated, having well over seven million residents. Because of limited space, especially on Hong Kong Island, the area abounds in an incredible number of closely-spaced skyscrapers, rising massively into the sky.

Around 1000 - 1400 CE, Chinese clans settled in what is now the New Territories. Hong Kong's deep and sheltered harbor promoted commerce early on. Trade between Hong Kong and Europe began in 1557, the year Portugal leased nearby Macau from China. In 1683, ships of the British East India Company arrived in Hong Kong and with them came the beginnings of British influence.

Some one hundred and fifty years later, trade issues between the British and the Chinese led to two conflicts, known as the Opium Wars. Britain was victorious in both conflicts. At the conclusion of the first war (1839 - 1842), China ceded Hong Kong Island to Britain in perpetuity. At the conclusion of the second war (1856 - 1860), China ceded Kowloon to Britain in perpetuity. And on July 1, 1898, China leased the New Territories to Britain for 99 years, ending on June 30, 1997. In 1911, the collapse of dynastic China was followed by the Communist Revolution and the Chinese Civil War (1945 - 1949). Establishment of the People's Republic of China by Mao Tse-Tung on October 1, 1949 resulted in a flood of refugees, both rich and poor, pouring into Hong Kong.

In 1982, as the end of the New Territories' lease loomed ahead, negotiations commenced between Britain and China regarding the return of all of Hong Kong to China. Legally, Britain was obligated to return only the New Territories, but by 1982 about half of Hong Kong's population lived in the New Territories and about half lived on Hong Kong Island and in Kowloon. Returning only the New Territories to China would have led to an unacceptable division of the region's population.

On June 30, 1997, Hong Kong reverted to China in accordance with a joint Sino-British declaration signed in 1984. China agreed to treat Hong Kong differently than the rest of the country for at least 50 years. It formulated a principle of "one country, two systems," and designated Hong Kong a Special Administrative Region (SAR). In so doing, China allowed Hong Kong's residents to enjoy a great measure of political independence and to conduct their business affairs under a capitalist system. At the same time, Hong Kong continued to function as a major international commerce and banking center and contributed immensely to China's finances through trade, manufacturing, and tourism.

*

All this was shattered on Thursday, July 5, 2029. As Hong Kong's residents awoke on that fateful day, sat down for breakfast, and prepared to go to work, they could not believe the news reports coming in over their radios and television sets. Stunned, they listened as reporters announced that in the early dawn a military escort had taken Jing Chong, Hong Kong's Chief Executive and Administrator, into custody. He and his family had been led out of their home and moved to an undisclosed location. At the same time, all local radio stations, TV networks, and newspapers were given an official communiqué which stated that the People's Republic of China (PRC) was revoking Hong Kong's SAR status, effective immediately. Jing Chong was replaced by Chao Tang, a firebrand ideologue of the PRC's Central Committee.

"After careful consideration," the communiqué explained, "the government of the People's Republic of China has concluded that the principle of 'one country, two systems' has shown itself to be utterly impractical. This idealistic and well-intentioned policy has given rise to a host of complications, frictions, and inconsistencies that have been detrimental to both the nation's economy and its socialist culture." The directive pointed out that it was unrealistic to expect a country as a whole to be able to function properly when an important region of that country embraced different political views (democratic concepts versus communist ideology), opposite economic systems (free markets versus state-controlled ones), varied banking rules, diverse cultural norms, and the like. "No other country in the world," the document said, "labors under such a handicap."

The communiqué then proceeded to give a second reason for revoking Hong Kong's SAR status. "Unfortunately," the document read, "Hong Kong's lax rules and permissive policies have made it an easy entry point and breeding ground for undesirable and extremist elements. These subversive groups have drawn on both foreign nationals and Chinese citizens. The former use Hong Kong for espionage activities against China and the latter foment counter-revolutionary thoughts and deeds. By letting such nefarious activities go on in its midst, Hong Kong has morphed into a threat to the entire country. Hence, China's security demands nothing less than the immediate dismantling of Hong Kong's preferential SAR status."

*

Hong Kong's response to China's abrogation of its contractual obligations under the Sino-British declaration was swift and powerful. Tens of thousands of Hong Kong Island residents dropped whatever they were doing, took to the streets, and converged on the Central Government Complex at Tamar Square on the island. They were joined by other tens of thousands who streamed onto Hong Kong Island from Kowloon and the New Territories, ferried across the water by Hong Kong's venerated Star Ferry. By day's end, a huge crowd had massed at Tamar Square—named after a British naval vessel that arrived in Hong Kong in 1897 and remained there until World War II—and spilled over into the neighborhood. Police in full riot gear guarded the perimeter of the complex, seat of Hong Kong's government since 2011. Observers estimated that as many as half a million protesters had converged on the complex.

As night fell, protesters camped out in the square and nearby streets. Throughout the night, the PRC brought in reinforcements of crack military units by boat and helicopter. As dawn broke, the police cordon attempted to push the crowd back. But the protesters did not budge. Police then resorted to tear gas.

People cowered and covered their faces, but did not move back. Heavily armed soldiers were deployed around the complex next. Loudspeakers and bullhorns warned the crowd to disperse or face live fire. Those in the back of the square and nearby streets had no intention of moving, while those closest to the complex were prevented from doing so by the pressure of the huge crowd pushing against them. When no movement of protesters ensued, the soldiers fired rubber bullets. Many protesters were wounded. Still the crowd refused to retreat. At that point, at precisely 11:30 am, the soldiers opened up with live fire aiming directly at the crowd, first targeting the front lines, then shooting as far as their weapons could reach. Front lines of protesters were mowed down, the dead and wounded piling up on top of each other. Many others fell, dead or injured, throughout the large throng of people. In no time was the square littered with corpses and screaming wounded. Blood drenched everything. Eye witnesses describe the scene as a ghastly slaughter, with hundreds having been killed or wounded. By some estimates, the number of casualties was over a thousand.

Terrorized, the crowd beat a retreat, but in the process casualties rose even higher as people were injured and trampled to their deaths by the stampede of the retreating protesters. The Tamar Square massacre, as it became known, was depressingly reminiscent of the infamous Tiananmen Square massacre, perpetrated by the Chinese government on June 4, 1989 in Beijing.

When the nightmare finally ended, an eerie quiet settled over the bloodied square. That evening China declared martial law for all of Hong Kong and imposed a strict overnight curfew. The draconian measures were imposed for a week, at which point an uneasy calm returned to the territory. How long it will last is anyone's guess.

Revulsion to the bloodbath has been widespread and ignited a firestorm of protests in front of Chinese embassies throughout the Free World. The loss of Hong Kong as an outpost of Western democracy and liberalism precipitated a flood of international actions targeting China. Britain recalled its ambassador from Beijing and suspended all diplomatic activity with China. The United States and many other western countries followed suit in short order. The UN Security Council put a condemnatory U.S.-sponsored resolution to a vote, but this was immediately vetoed by China, a permanent member of the Council. The imposition of sanctions on China was discussed by the European Union, NATO (North Atlantic Treaty Organization), and SEATO (Southeast Asia Treaty Organization). Agreement was reached on some minor sanctions but not on major crippling ones. In all three forums there were some countries that were reluctant to sacrifice their economic ties with China by supporting powerful sanctions. Their economic concerns overruled moral and political considerations. The lack of unity among the world's democracies in fighting aggression has been worrisome.

*

In 1997 some observers had hoped that granting Hong Kong SAR status would ultimately lead China to become more like Hong Kong, but others feared that the opposite would occur. Moreover, they felt that the central government's takeover of Hong Kong was inevitable and that it was not a question of *if* but rather one of *when*. Events have proven these observers to have been correct on all counts.

When China violated its contractual obligation by revoking Macau's SAR status on September 10, 2024, the action generated only a weak response, both domestically and internationally. Analysts warned at the time that lack of a powerful response to violations of international agreements always emboldens the aggressor to commit further, and more devastating, acts of aggression. Loss of the SAR status, first for Macau and now for Hong Kong, is a case in point. Regrettably it corroborates the insight of Aldous Huxley, who said *That men do not learn very much from history is the most important lesson that history has to teach.*

The Hermit Nation Runs Amok

WORLD VIEW

By James Morrison

June 22, 2031

SEOUL, South Korea—North Korea has engaged frequently in asymmetric warfare with the West and especially with the United States. Typically, this type of warfare occurs between two belligerents who differ markedly in their military strength. In such cases, the weaker belligerent resorts to strategies (provocative, intimidating, deceitful) that, despite the adversary's deficiency, produce results that the adversary seeks. Manifestations of North Korea's asymmetric warfare have occurred repeatedly over the years, but in the last two months their scope has increased in both frequency and intensity. North Korea fired several missiles across the Sea of Japan, harassing both Japanese and South Korean fishing boats. When two boats were actually hit and sunk (with loss of life), North Korea claimed that the boats had strayed into its territorial waters and had ignored repeated warnings to withdraw. Additionally, North Korea dispatched drones over key military installations in South Korea. One drone was shot down and found to have been equipped with powerful cameras. There were also a number of incidents involving the country's nuclear power program. A new uranium processing plant has commenced operation despite objection by the International Atomic Energy Agency. And three times the regime made preparations to conduct a nuclear test, but each time the test was aborted at the last minute. As usual, the asymmetric warfare incidents were followed by the regime attempting to extort political or economic concessions, including financial aid. The Pentagon ascribed the increase in North Korea's asymmetric warfare to the need the regime apparently had for such theatrics in order to maintain a firm grip on its citizenry. This interpretation was supported by the fact that, of late, there had been known shake-ups in the regime as well as rumors about the inability of the current Great Leader to retain control. Having viewed the increase in belligerence in this light, Western leaders did not find it necessary to respond forcefully to the various provocations.

*

That line of reasoning was discarded abruptly when, a week ago, fighting broke out between North and South Korea at the Demilitarized Zone (DMZ), the strip of land that is the border between the two countries. Suddenly it became clear that North Korea's two month-long belligerence must have had two purposes. First, the belligerence would allow North Korea to gauge the

West's readiness and willingness to react forcefully to provocations. The lack of such a response could then be taken as a green light for the country to continue with its planned aggression. Second, the asymmetric warfare would divert the West's attention and keep the West from discovering North Korea's secret preparation for an all-out assault on South Korea. In particular, it would allow North Korea to complete construction of two new, all-important infiltration tunnels, dug deep under the DMZ, and ready them for breakout.

The confrontation started when, in the pre-dawn hours of June 16, 2031, two squads of North Korean soldiers materialized south of the Military Demarcation Line (MDL), the line that runs through the middle of the DMZ. The soldiers had emerged from the two newly constructed infiltration tunnels and were advancing toward the South Korean positions. As soon as they were spotted, South Korean guards fired warning shots. When the North Koreans continued to advance, the guards shot at them with all the fire power at their command. The North Korean soldiers returned fire, but were mowed down by volleys of bullets coming at them from the other side. At that point all hell broke loose. Later some people speculated that the North may well have intentionally orchestrated a suicide-type mission for the two squads to be used as a pretext for a full-fledged assault on the South. Whatever the explanation, wave after wave of North Korean soldiers poured out of the two tunnels. They were heavily armed and attacked the South Korean positions with a vengeance. At the same time, North Korea launched barrages of mortars and rockets which streaked across the border into South Korea, and North Korean fighter planes scrambled into the air and screamed overhead. Anti-tank walls and other barriers in the DMZ were blown up to create paths for the hundreds of tanks and armored personnel carriers massed on the North Korean side. While fighting raged at the DMZ, North Korean missile patrol boats and attack submarines began shelling South Korea at Inch'on on the west coast and at Pusan on the south coast, apparently as a prelude to a planned invasion.

*

The roots of the Korean conflict date to the end of World War II. In August 1945, the Soviet Union declared war on Japan and poured troops into Korea, which had been occupied and ruled by Japan since 1910. On August 11, U.S. officials proposed a temporary division of Korea to prevent a complete takeover of the entire peninsula by the Soviets. Specifically, they proposed establishing a Soviet military zone north of the 38th parallel and an American military zone south of it. The Soviets accepted the proposal.

Subsequently, these two zones became two independent nations, South Korea (the Republic of Korea, ROK), established

August 11, 1948, with Seoul as its capital, and North Korea (the Democratic People's Republic of Korea, DPRK), established September 9, 1948, with Pyongyang as its capital. Each nation occupied roughly one half of the peninsula. As time went on, contrast between the two countries could not have become any starker. South Korea evolved into a modern democratic state, boasting of a flourishing economy, a vibrant culture, and a people who cherished their freedom. North Korea, on the other hand, degenerated into a brutal police state, with thousands of its people in gulags and horrid prisons. The country became an international pariah, having few contacts with the outside world, subsisting on a collapsed economy, committing the worst human rights violations on the planet, and spending all its efforts and money on building an ever more threatening war machine.

*

On June 25, 1950, North Korea launched a well-planned attack on South Korea in an attempt to unify the country. A large military force equipped with Soviet tanks crossed the 38th parallel. President Truman sent American troops (later augmented by UN forces) to Korea to stop the North Korean aggression. Thus began the Korean War which lasted three years. An armistice was finally signed on July 27, 1953, but there has never been a formal end to the war.

With the armistice came the establishment of the DMZ, the current border between South and North Korea. The DMZ runs from east to west, is 160 miles long and 2.5 miles wide, and straddles the 38th parallel. Despite its name, a powerful imprint is pervasive on both sides of the DMZ making it the most heavily fortified and most dangerous strip of land in the world. The DMZ is studded with barriers, security devices, and armaments of all kinds: mines, gun emplacements, electrified fences, anti-tank walls, automated turrets, sensors, listening devices, optical scanners, robot patrols, radar installations, jamming and communication towers, live patrols, and guards whose binoculars are constantly trained on the opposite side. In effect, two powerful militaries stare at each other across the DMZ. In 2015, South Korea had over 600,000 men on active duty (augmented by 28,000 U.S. troops), while North Korea had 1,100,000 men on active duty. Both countries have additional millions of soldiers in reserve and paramilitary units. With this staggering number of troops facing each other, the DMZ has become a tinderbox that could, as it just did, blow up in a flash.

Notwithstanding the fortress nature of the DMZ there have been numerous incidents along it over the years, most until now relatively minor. Among the incidents were the discoveries of four tunnels dug by North Korea under the zone. The tunnels were dug at great depth, about 200-450 ft below ground, were long (about 6,000 - 9,000 ft), wide (about 6 ft), and high (about 6 ft). North Korea claimed that the tunnels were part of its mining operations, but no residues of such operations were ever found. The tunnels' large size suggested that they were designed to serve as infiltration routes since each tunnel could support the transit of more than 30,000 troops, three to four abreast, with field artillery, in one hour.

*

That this was the intended use of the underground tunnels was borne out by discovery of the two newly constructed tunnels through which North Korean troops poured and infiltrated South Korea a week ago. As of this writing, fighting is still raging all along the DMZ as well as inland at Inch'on and Pusan. North Korea claims that its soldiers had emerged into the DMZ north of the MDL and thus were clearly in North Korean territory. They considered the killing of their men by the South Korean border guards an act of war that justified their powerful response. They say that they are determined to unify the two countries once and for all, and bring the entire Korean peninsula under their control. It looks for all intents and purposes as if a second Korean War has just broken out. The big question is what will the United States do? Legally, it is bound to come to the defense of South Korea having signed a Mutual Defense Treaty and a Mutual Defense Pact with it in 1954 and 2013, respectively. But do the American people have the stomach for another Korean war? And will the U.S. government honor its obligation or will it throw another ally under the proverbial bus, as has happened elsewhere? The even bigger question is what will North Korea do if it is successfully repulsed? Will it resort to its arsenal of weapons of mass destruction—chemical, biological, and nuclear? With all its past theatrics involving nuclear weapons, will it really pull the trigger now and catapult the world into a potential Armageddon?

A Landmark Decision

WORLD VIEW

By Michael Burns

September 21, 2031

WASHINGTON, DC—On September 15, 2031, the *Alliance for the Advancement of Christian Ethics and Family Values* scored a major victory when the Supreme Court of the United States ruled in favor of Berry in *Kemp v. Berry*.

The *Alliance*, as it is commonly referred to, is a Washington, DC-based organization that has grown out of *The Family*. The latter, a more or less covert organization, was founded in the 1930s. Its religious character and its hobnobbing with the rich and powerful have been described in detail by Jeff Sharlet in two books: *The Family - The Secret Fundamentalism at the Heart of American Power* (2009), and *C Street - The Fundamentalist Threat to American Democracy* (2010). The Alliance was established in 2020 to weigh in openly against the perceived increasing secularism of the United States. In the ensuing years, the Alliance has grown from humble beginnings, a coalition of three like-minded associations (The Family, Christian Morals Unlimited, and American Family Values) to become a political powerhouse that serves as an umbrella organization for virtually all of the Religious Right groups of the country. Numerous and diverse bodies—Baptist brotherhoods, evangelical associations, Catholic coalitions, right-to-life societies, Bible fellowships, and others—operate under the aegis of the Alliance. Briefly stated, the organization's aim is to make the United States into an openly Christian nation, one that embodies a God-fearing, Jesus-centered society. Over the years, the organization has recruited and groomed a large number of prominent individuals to become future activists in the Alliance. Among them have been key congressional senators and representatives, heads of governmental departments and agencies, top brass of the military, CEOs of major corporations, and many of the wealthiest individuals in the country. It is an open secret that the Alliance's unabashed support for Republican candidate Ralph Prescott played a major role in assuring his 2028 election as President of the United States.

*

Once the dust had settled after the election, the Alliance's leadership realized that the time was opportune to advance the organization's agenda aggressively. The immediate target was the First Amendment of the Constitution, the interpretation of which had been a bone of contention for decades. Both proponents and opponents of the wall of separation between church and state have always attempted to bolster their position by reference to the First Amendment. The Alliance was determined to have its view of church and state prevail and to achieve that via a Supreme Court ruling. Fortuitously, the case of *Kemp v. Berry* was just then moving through the lower courts. Harry Kemp, president of the Indiana chapter of Americans United for Separation of Church and State, had sued George Berry, a widely-known evangelical minister who headed a mega-church in Indianapolis, IN. The suit alleged that Berry had blatantly endorsed Religious Right candidates for the 2028 election from the pulpit. His violation of the prohibition on politicizing the pulpit had included an impassioned endorsement of soon-to-be President Prescott.

The Alliance threw its support behind Berry and saw to it that the case was dealt with swiftly. In February 2030, it ended up on the Supreme Court's docket. At that time the court had a majority of right-wing judges, three of whom had been active in the Alliance prior to their nomination. Hence, the Alliance had ready-made access to the court where it exerted its influence to the fullest. On September 15, 2031, the Supreme Court, in a seven to two decision, ruled in favor of George Berry. The judicial majority opined that ministers and other clergy were well within their constitutional rights to engage in political activity from the pulpit. The judges' statement declared that "political expression is a matter of free speech and clergy, like every other citizen, must be allowed to voice their political preferences, including making specific political endorsements."

*

Momentous as the above decision was, it became even more far-reaching as a result of unprecedented action then taken by the Supreme Court. In a radical departure from established practice, the court decided to extend its ruling from the specific case at hand to the general issue of religious expression, thereby taking a firm stand on the interpretation of the First Amendment. The strongly-worded majority opinion read in part that "we feel that *Kemp v. Berry* goes to the core issue of religious expression. While we have addressed the right of clergy to give vent to their religious beliefs through political activism, we must also address the right of any citizen to give vent to his/her religious beliefs, be it through political activism or in some other way. Therefore, while we agree that the intent of the First Amendment is to assure that government does not interfere with religious expression, we also read it to mean that no citizen, regardless of the public or private office he/she holds, should be barred from openly expressing his/her religious beliefs, be it in speech, writing, display, practice, or in any other form."

Thus, *Kemp v. Berry* came to be a landmark decision that put to rest the controversy about the First Amendment and that changed life in the United States by effectively tearing down the wall of separation between church and state. The very broad license allowed those holding public office to actively, and openly, pursue faith-driven agendas. The flood gates having been thrown wide open, it is to be expected that activists will unleash a torrent of changes thereby remaking the fabric of American society for generations to come.

An Environmental Update

WORLD VIEW

By Michael Burns

August 7, 2033

NEW YORK, NY—Every year the Economic and Social Council (ECOSOC) of the United Nations holds a month-long session in July in either Geneva or New York. The Council deals with economic, social, and environmental matters and is a central platform of the United Nations for debate and innovative thinking. The session just concluded was held in New York and was devoted entirely to a discussion of climate change. Presentations made by experts from around the globe painted a dismal picture of the world's environment. There was broad consensus that failure to address global warming effectively and in a timely fashion had caught up with the earth. But there was less agreement about what the world could do at this point to forestall further catastrophic events and to try and restore earlier, more favorable climatic conditions. Several reports presented at the ECOSOC session are summarized below.

*

Both the southwestern part of the United States and the Great Plains have been laboring under a severe drought that is now in its seventh year. A drought that lasts ten years or more is known as a mega-drought. This one is well on its way to becoming one and no one knows when it will end. Experts had predicted that there was an almost one hundred percent chance that a mega-drought would occur in the United States between 2050 and 2100. What they had not anticipated was that the accelerated deterioration of the global climate might actually bring on such a drought much earlier. So far, the drought has been especially pronounced in Arizona, California, Kansas, New Mexico, Oklahoma, and Texas. In these states, agriculture has been dealt a mortal blow, local economies have been severely depressed, and tourism has largely ceased. Though the land had been farmed properly in the past to avoid a repetition of the 1930s dust bowl, the prolonged drought has undermined these efforts. Intense heat, wildfires, wind erosion, a dearth of precipitation, and ongoing human activity on the parched land have all combined to generate loose topsoil that spreads across the states in the form of debilitating sand storms. Over the past seven years there have been at least 525 deaths that have been blamed on the drastic weather conditions.

*

The northeastern part of the United States has also had its share of extreme weather conditions. For several years now, winters in that part of the country have been extraordinarily severe. Wave after wave of arctic air has blasted the region for extended periods with temperatures of -5 F to -10 F and wind chill factors of -30 to -40. There have been lengthy blizzards, blinding white-outs, and dangerous freezing rain and ice storms. Numerous accidents have occurred on snow and ice covered roads and highways. Both Boston and Buffalo have been buried repeatedly under mountains of snow, 6 - 8 ft tall. Frequently, after the region had barely recovered from the travails of a severe winter, it was pummeled by one or more powerful hurricanes. Both the number and severity of these storms have increased markedly. Most damaging of all was Juliet, a category 4 hurricane that struck New York City in the fall of 2030 with wind gusts of 140 miles per hour and storm surges of 18 feet. Two million people in the city and its environs lost power, subway routes were flooded, and streets were littered with broken glass from shattered skyscraper windows. The storm brought the Big Apple to a standstill for three days, and the devastation left in its track ran into a billion dollars.

*

Europe has not been spared catastrophic climatic events either. In the summer of 2029 Europe experienced another deadly heat wave reminiscent of the one that paralyzed the continent in 2003 from mid-June to mid-August and killed more than 35,000 people. This one lasted almost 13 weeks (from June 4 through September 1) and affected a large area that stretched from the Mediterranean to the Baltic and from the North Atlantic to the Black Sea. The only countries escaping the heat wave were the United Kingdom, Ireland, the Scandinavian countries, and Russia. The rest of Europe sweltered under continuous high temperatures which frequently rose to 105 F. Forest fires were widespread in Germany, France, Portugal, and Spain, and runoff from glaciers in the Alps created massive flooding in both Switzerland and Austria. The heat wave was more severe than the 2003 one, lasted longer and resulted in a higher death toll. An estimated 40,000 - 45,000 people died from the broiling heat. Most of the casualties were either elderly or the very young.

*

Flooding in Bangladesh is practically an integral part of the people's way of life. The country is relatively flat, with the southern and southeastern coastal terrain at sea level, and two thirds of the inland area less than 17 ft above sea level. As such, Bangladesh is extremely vulnerable to the devastating action of monsoons and cyclones, not to mention tsunamis. The country lies at the foot of the Himalayas and most of the snowmelt from these mountains flows through Bangladesh on its way to the sea. The snowmelt feeds two mighty rivers, Ganges and Brahmaputra, and numerous tributaries. The multitude of rivers and the low elevation of the land make Bangladesh effectively a delta in a flood plain. In the dry season, about one third of the country is covered with water; during the rainy season (which coincides with the snow-melting season) about two thirds of the country is under water. In recent years, floods, monsoons, and cyclones have become more numerous, longer-lasting, and more severe. Powerful storms and rising sea levels have destroyed crops by flooding rice paddies with salt water. The country has made great strides to minimize cyclone damage by improving early warning systems and constructing concrete storm shelters. Thus, while cyclone Bhola in 1970 killed 550,000, and cyclone 1991 killed 138,000, cyclone Aila in 2009 killed "only" 300 people. The most recent climatic catastrophe was a terrifying cyclone that struck the country in April 2028 (dubbed Cyclone 2028). It posted winds of 145 miles per hour and storm surges of 19 - 32 ft and was equivalent to a category 5 hurricane. The entire southern and southeastern coastlines were ravaged by the storm. Two major cities, Patuakhali on the southern coast and Chittagong on the southeastern coast, reported devastating damage. Despite the country's precautionary measures, the death toll climbed once again to a level not seen for many years. There were 12,000 confirmed deaths, but officials estimate that in actuality 18,000 people may have perished in the catastrophic event.

*

One of the few bright spots of the ECOSOC session was a report by a representative of the Desertec Foundation. This foundation had been established on January 20, 2009 to promote the use of abundant sources of renewable energy throughout the world: (1) Concentrated solar thermal power in desert regions; (2) Wind power in coastal areas; (3) Hydroelectric power in mountainous regions; (4) Photovoltaic solar panels in sunny areas; and (5) Biomass and geothermal power where appropriate. The Desertec Industrial Initiative (Dii) is a consortium of twelve major and powerful European companies that was founded on October 30, 2009 to implement the goals of the Desertec Foundation. The original project envisioned using the solar energy striking the Sahara desert to generate electric power, which would then be transmitted to consumption centers in Europe via long-distance cables. However, technical difficulties, insufficient funding, and lack of cooperation by African countries led the Dii to abandon the Sahara project in 2013.

The exciting news that the Foundation representative brought to the session was that the Sahara project had been revived three years ago, in March 2030. Four factors have made this possible. First, six major new companies have joined the consortium, thereby providing much-needed additional and critical expertise. Second, important technological breakthroughs—unique new photovoltaic solar panels, revolutionary steam turbines powered by the sun's heat, improved cable grids for power transmission, etc.—have been achieved during the preceding years that make the Sahara project much more feasible. Third, Dii has been successful in securing substantial financial backing from the World Bank and from both governmental and private sources in Germany, the United Kingdom, and France. And fourth, a number of African countries have come forward and declared their intent to cooperate in the multinational undertaking. Specifically, they have donated land outright to the project and offered Dii low-cost, long-term leases for other areas. In return, Dii has agreed to divert a portion of the generated electric power to these countries where it would be used to run sea water desalination plants to alleviate chronic water shortages. With all this in place, it looks as if the ambitious Sahara Desertec project is well on its way toward implementation.

Heeding the Call

WORLD VIEW

By Michael Burns

October 1, 2034

NEW YORK, NY—Last month was the three-year anniversary of the Supreme Court's *Kemp v. Berry* landmark decision, which effectively tore down the wall of separation between church and state in the United States. That decision, rendered on September 15, 2031, read in part that "no citizen, regardless of the public or private office he/she holds, should be barred from openly expressing his/her religious beliefs, be it in speech, writing, display, practice, or in any other form." The decision produced an avalanche of changes in both public and private life.

President Ralph Prescott, an ardent evangelical, was among the first to show what the new ruling made possible for those holding public office. Soon after the Supreme Court announced its ruling, Prescott modified the White House decor. A bronze sculpture of the Ten Commandments now graced the Oval Office to remind him of his and the country's Judeo-Christian heritage. Additionally, a number of large religious paintings (a manger scene, the Last Supper, the crucifixion of Jesus, and others) were hung throughout the White House. Later on, Prescott instituted other changes. At Christmas, he had a large luminous cross installed on top of the presidential Christmas tree on the White House lawn and a magnificent nativity scene erected nearby. And, at both Christmas and Easter, the president addressed the nation in a kind of fireside chat, stressing the importance of religious beliefs and family values.

Many state governors took their cue from the president. With support from their legislatures, they had religious displays erected at state capitols. By far the favorite display was a Ten Commandments tablet, either as carved wood, sculpted stone, or welded metal. During the Christmas season, striking nativity scenes were erected in front of state capitols and colorful religious banners adorned the surrounding grounds.

Congress instituted a new event, modeled after the popular annual National Prayer Breakfast. The latter had been held every February in the Hilton in Washington, DC since the 1980s. Typically, some three thousand guests attended the event, including the president, members of Congress, and leaders from the United States and abroad. The congressional Republican majority, desirous of keeping the spirit of the breakfast alive throughout the year, voted to hold a similar event during the summer months. This second gathering, called Congressional Prayer Breakfast, was organized and hosted entirely by congressional Republicans. It was smaller than the February event because guests were limited almost exclusively to members of Congress and the administration, and it was timed for the return of Congress from its Independence Day recess. The first Congressional Prayer Breakfast was held in June 2032.

*

Over the years quite a few changes have been introduced that affect the general public. Job applications nowadays usually require disclosure of one's religious affiliation, and candidates for public office are invariably questioned at length about their religious persuasion. Religious organizations are at liberty to restrict their hiring to coreligionists without having to fear lawsuits charging discrimination. The use of vouchers for education has been federally mandated, but the details of voucher administration vary from state to state. The number of parochial schools in the country has mushroomed and many receive outright government support. Following a directive from President Prescott, the U.S. Department of Education assessed the state of education in the nation's public high schools. In line with its mission to identify problem areas and make recommendations for dealing with them, the department concluded that public high schools were delinquent in providing students with ample possibilities to participate in the nation's embrace of open religious expression. While adults were able to do so with ease, students spent a good part of each day in an environment in which religious expression was essentially banned. To rectify this, the department recommended that schools take three remedial steps: (1) Have principals offer a prayer, referred to as a *spiritual invitation*, over the public address system at the beginning of the school day; (2) Encourage students to deliver prayers, characterized as *inspirational messages*, at school assemblies; (3) Offer a course on religion, covering the Christian underpinnings of America from the pilgrims to modern times.

The Dragon Spews Fire

WORLD VIEW

By James Morrison

June 10, 2035

TAIPEI, Taiwan—The Far East is in turmoil! At the center of the storm is Taiwan, a small island of 14,000 square miles, shaped like a leaf and located in the Taiwan Strait some 100 miles east of mainland China. The island is home to 23 million people, passionate about their democracy and proud of their vibrant economy. All that came under attack on June 5, 2035.

On that fateful day, the People's Republic of China (PRC) launched a full-scale invasion of the island to force it to accept complete reunification with the mainland. It was a complex operation of three coordinated campaigns: first, a massive amphibious attack on the less densely populated section of Taiwan's western coast, about midway between Tainan and Taichung, with the goal of establishing a beachhead; second, missile strikes and bombing raids on major air bases, radar installations and communication facilities aimed at degrading Taiwan's defenses and immobilizing its government; and third, cyber warfare against Taiwan's political, military, and economic infrastructure designed to intimidate the population by inducing fear and loss of confidence in the country's leadership.

The invasion came three months after China had declared the waters around Taiwan to be live-fire training zones, so as to discourage ships from entering Taiwan ports. In effect, the strategy amounted to a form of naval blockade. At the same time, China made it known that it would be willing to consider granting Taiwan a status similar to that of the Special Administrative Region (SAR) it had granted Macau and Hong Kong previously. Not surprisingly, in light of China's unilateral abrogation of those two treaties, the people of Taiwan had little interest in pursuing that option. When the PRC's offer was turned down, a thinly-veiled threat was added to the "blockade." Specifically, China stated publicly that Taiwan's current political status cannot continue indefinitely. Eventually, the island must be reunited with the mainland so that the PRC can exercise its legitimate control over all of the parts that together comprise the historic Chinese nation.

As of this writing, almost a week into the invasion, China has successfully secured a beachhead on Taiwan's western coast. This allowed it to bring ashore troops, tanks, armored vehicles, and other armaments and dispatch them inland as needed. Fierce battles are currently raging around Taipei and Keelung in the north, Taichung and Chiayi in the center, Kaohsiung in the southwest, and Taitung in the southeast. A large Chinese naval force surrounds the island, with two aircraft carriers, the *Beijing* and the *Shanghai* stationed north and south of the island, respectively. Missile and bombing raids have caused significant physical damage while cyber warfare has made part of the country's infrastructure inoperative.

*

International condemnation of China's naked aggression has been vociferous and wide-spread. The UN Security Council met in an emergency session, but other than heated verbal exchanges the Council was unable to offer anything else. All proposed resolutions were immediately vetoed by China and Russia, both permanent members of the Council. Moreover, China stressed to the Council that it had all the legal authority needed for military intervention in what its representative referred to as a "police action against a rebel province."

Readers of this column will recall the international paralysis that followed China's revocation of Macau's and Hong Kong's SAR status. Much the same transpired this time around. The imposition of sanctions on China was discussed by the European Union, NATO (North Atlantic Treaty Organization), and SEATO (Southeast Asia Treaty Organization). But once again, as happened before, these talks produced only mixed results. While agreement was reached on imposition of minor sanctions, there was no consensus regarding truly crippling sanctions. Several member countries of the European Union and NATO were reluctant to sacrifice their economic ties with China by supporting such sanctions. And most members of SEATO refused to support major sanctions for fear of alienating China—a superpower in their immediate vicinity—and provoking it to commit acts of aggression against their own countries. Even Japan, though it viewed the possibility of the Taiwan Strait becoming an internal Chinese waterway with great concern, voted against the imposition of crippling sanctions.

Only the United States, which has a special relationship with Taiwan, made a concrete move. It ordered two aircraft carriers and three destroyers, all part of the Seventh Fleet and stationed in the Pacific, to steam toward the Taiwan Strait. Whether or not the U.S. will go to war to stop the invasion is not known. The situation is complex. The United States has been playing a balancing act characterized by strategic ambiguity. On the one hand, Washington has courted Beijing and engaged in extensive economic relations, not the least of which has been to become China's main debtor nation. On the other hand, Washington has remained Taiwan's principal ally, providing it with arms and pledged to come to its aid in the event of an attack. The latter is codified in the Taiwan Relations Act (TRA) of 1979 (Public Law 96-8, 96th Congress). According to the TRA, the United States is committed to "maintain the capacity of the United States to resist any resort to force or other forms of coercion that would jeopardize the security, or the social or economic system, of the people on Taiwan." The act further stipulates that the United States will "consider any effort to determine the future of Taiwan by other than peaceful means, including boycotts or embargoes, a threat to the peace and security of the Western Pacific area and of grave concern to the United States." What will happen when the vessels of the Seventh Fleet reach the Taiwan Strait is anyone's guess. Conceivably, arrival of the ships could be the start of the long threatened and dangerous military confrontation between China and the United States for control of Southeast Asia.

*

To understand the roots of the China-Taiwan conflict, one has to go back in time and review Taiwan's turbulent history. Prior to arrival of Europeans, indigenous people had lived on Taiwan for thousands of years. Most probably came from Southeast Asia and Polynesia, but the 1400s also saw immigrants arriving from China's Fujian province. From the 14th to the 16th century, Chinese and Japanese pirates used Taiwan as a stronghold and safe haven. Europeans first arrived in the area in the middle of the 16th century. A Portuguese fleet is believed to have "discovered" Taiwan in 1542. Impressed by the island's green and mountainous terrain they named it Ilha Formosa, meaning "Beautiful Island." Hence, for several centuries, the island was known as Formosa.

The Dutch arrived in the early part of the 17th century and Taiwan became an important trading center for the Dutch East India Company. But in the mid 17th century China took control of Taiwan and the Qing dynasty ruled it for some 200 years. After China lost the Sino-Japanese war of 1894 it ceded Taiwan to Japan, which ruled it till after World War II. In 1945 Taiwan was officially restored to China by the Allied powers. In October of that year, the Chinese installed a brutal administrator, Chen Yi, and Taiwanese soon felt they had merely traded one oppressive colonial government (Japanese) for another (Chinese). An uprising of the people on February 27, 1947 was followed the next day by a massacre, known as the 228 incident.

After World War II, the Nationalists had been fighting the Communists in China. When Mao Tse-Tung, leader of the Communists, proclaimed the People's Republic of China (PRC) in 1949, Chiang Kai-Shek, leader of the Nationalists, fled to Taiwan. There he set up the Nationalists as a government in exile with himself at the head. He ruled Taiwan from 1949 until 1974. Chiang instituted liberal economic reforms and prepared the ground for Taiwan's remarkable economic growth in the years to come. At the same time, however, he ruled with a heavy hand, curtailed political freedom, banned opposition parties, and placed Taiwan under martial law. After Chiang's death in 1975, conditions improved marginally, but significant change and transition to democracy only came with the advent of Lee Teng-Hui who rose to power in 1988. Lee, often called the "Father of Taiwan's Democracy," instituted democratic reforms and legalized opposition parties. Taiwan's first direct election of president took place in 1996 and Lee was elected by an overwhelming majority. An advocate of independence, Lee declared that China and Taiwan were two separate states.

*

Considering this background, it is easy to appreciate the despair that gripped Taiwan when China launched its invasion. Taiwan's road to independence had been long, arduous, and studded with obstacles. Consequently, citizens were passionate about their hard-won freedom and determined to defend it at all costs, no matter the sacrifice. If they had to go down, they would do so fighting. They looked to the United States to come to their aid in this hour of need as it had committed itself to do over and over again for decades.

Many analysts have said for a long time that China's grab of Taiwan was inevitable, that it was not a question of *if*, but rather one of *when*. This view gained additional adherents after China's revocation of SAR status, first for Macau and then for Hong

Kong. Invading Taiwan seemed to be an almost natural sequel to these two violations of international agreements. Nor did the analysts have any delusions as to the timing of the invasion. They predicted that it would occur when the United States, the only superpower standing in the way, would show signs of weakness and/or detachment from Southeast Asia. Unfortunately, these developments have now come about.

The much-touted pivot to Asia of American policy, first announced by the Obama administration, had never taken off. In fact, the opposite had occurred. America had retreated from pressure points in Asia much as it had retreated from pressure points elsewhere around the globe. On the whole, the United States was now being viewed by both friend and foe as a paper tiger, ignoring its own threats and deadlines, with even its internal cocoon in disarray. Many allies have lost confidence and trust in America. Additionally, America had become extremely war-weary. Having fought five wars—Korea, Vietnam, Iraq (twice), and Afghanistan—which had cost thousands of lives, even more thousands of wounded (physically and/or mentally), and untold billions of dollars, the country had no inclination for engaging in another war, especially one with a rising superpower like China. Given these conditions, China calculated that if it ever were to make the move to take over Taiwan, now was as good a time as any. China apparently believed that it could act with impunity and avoid a confrontation with the United States. So far, the imminent arrival of the ships from the U.S. Seventh Fleet does not seem to have brought about a change in China's basic calculation. There has been no letup of China's attack on Taiwan.

So Taiwan must confront a very unpleasant reality. Neither the United States nor anyone else is likely to come to its rescue. Considering China's overwhelming military superiority, there is little doubt about the outcome of this conflict. It is most likely that China's might will trounce that of Taiwan in a short time and that the mainland power will succeed in subduing the island nation and exacting its complete capitulation. The resultant new political reality would constitute a very sad ending to the brave, 400-year-old struggle of the Taiwanese for independence.

An Old Controversy

WORLD VIEW

By Michael Burns

October 28, 2035

BERKELEY, CA—On October 18, 2035, the U.S. Department of Education, in line with its mission to identify and deal with curriculum issues in public high schools, released a directive urging high schools to revamp their biology curricula. "From now on," the directive read, "all public high schools are herewith instructed to teach the latest version of creationism side-by-side with the theory of evolution, and to treat them as equivalent scientific theories." The directive reflected recent polls which had shown that 75% of Americans believed creationism, rather than Darwinian evolution, provided the best explanation for the origin of life on earth. How the U.S. Department of Education had arrived at its position makes for quite a story.

*

The first major conflict between proponents of evolution and proponents of creationism can be dated to the famous Scopes trial (monkey trial) of July 10-21, 1925, held in Dayton, Tennessee. This was followed by emergence of the Creation Research Society in 1963, establishment of the Institute for Creation Research in 1970, fashioning of the Intelligent Design Movement in the 1980s and, most recently, founding of the American Society for Intelligent Design (ASID) in 2025. ASID replaced all previous creationist groups and its name was intended to show that it was on a par with other scientific American societies. ASID was governed by a board of directors, with Ronald Morton as its current charismatic chairman.

Morton was aware of the increased religious activism that had been spreading across the country following the Supreme Court's *Kemp v. Berry* ruling of September 15, 2031, which opened the door to public religious expression. The changed landscape, he felt, made it opportune for him to advance a bold new version of creationism he had been developing for some time. And so, in December 2032, during a lengthy interview by Jim Kagan of CNN, he made a bombshell announcement.

In essence, he proposed a new theory, which he dubbed "Quantum Evolution." In this, he took his cue from the Quantum Theory that had revolutionized physics and chemistry at the beginning of the twentieth century. The term Quantum, coined by Max Planck in 1900, described a discrete natural unit—a packet or bundle—of energy, charge, or some other physical property. Planck proposed that atoms emit and absorb energy not in a continuous manner, but rather in the form of quanta. By analogy, Morton argued, evolutionary changes do occur, but only in the form of what he termed quantum leaps. In what appeared to be a complete shift in the creationist position, Morton conceded that Darwin and other biological scientists had been correct in asserting that some changes occur in living systems. Where they had gone wrong, he explained, was in assuming that these changes constituted a continuum, an unbroken spectrum, that allowed one species to evolve into another. Much as the physicists had been wrong in assuming that energy emission and absorption by atoms proceeded in a continuous manner, so biologists had been wrong in assuming that evolution proceeded in a continuous manner. Evolutionary changes do occur, but only in the form of quantum leaps. Morton stated that quantum evolution was a modern outgrowth of the antiquated concepts of Darwinian evolution. The latter, he maintained, had never been embraced by a majority of the people. But the former, he said, provided a clear interpretation that everyone could accept.

"Put somewhat differently," he elaborated, "small changes within a species do take place. People grow taller because of better nutrition; they live longer because of better health care; sleep cycles may change as society becomes more technologically oriented; domesticated animals may lose their hunger for raw meat. And so on and so forth. Such minor changes merely result in accentuation of individual differences; they can never result in conversion of one species into another. That requires a major change, a quantum leap. And quantum leaps can only be carried out by an omnipotent creator."

"The first and most important quantum leap occurred," he added, "when God, having created apes, decided to create human beings. Now, whether the Creator used actual monkey bones and flesh as starting material or whether he fashioned human bodies from simpler elements is irrelevant. What God created—humans—was something entirely new, even if they were constructed from monkey parts. The important point is that these humans were the handiwork of the Creator; they could not have come about in any other way. If evolutionists want to argue that man 'derived' from apes because apes came first and man came later, so be it. But the appearance of man after apes reflects a quantum leap that could have been orchestrated only by divine power."

*

As word spread about the new thrust of creationism, journalists pounced on the story. Bold headlines declared: "Quantum Evolution—the truth about creation;" "Reconciliation of evolution and creationism;" "Darwin and God meet at last." As time went on, Morton began to refer to members of ASID as Quantum Evolution Darwinists. The term caught on and was abbreviated as Q.E.D. The abbreviation normally stands for the Latin phrase "quod erat demonstrandum" (which was to be demonstrated) and is used to indicate the successful conclusion of a mathematical proof. Placed at the end of a derivation, it signifies that the proof has been established. Morton's use of Q.E.D. implied that Quantum Evolution Darwinists were the last, definitive step in the long debate. They brought the evolution controversy to its successful conclusion. The proof had been established. Q.E.D.

Q.E.D. became the buzzword for these creationist "reformers" of the biological sciences. Before long, a monthly magazine appeared titled *Q.E.D. News*. An easy-to-read format, glossy paper, and vivid colors combined to produce attractive issues. The magazine was geared to adults and featured nature photography, creation science news, inspirational articles, and poetry. *Q.E.D. News* became a publishing success rivaling that of the *National Geographic* magazine.

When the concept of quantum evolution was first proposed, scientists had greeted it with derision. Bemused at the concept's irrationality—yes evolution, no evolution—and at Morton's mix of fact and fiction, they had assumed that quantum evolution would soon disappear from the scene. When they realized their error, it was too late to reverse the trend. By the summer of 2035, quantum evolution had become firmly entrenched throughout the United States. All that was lacking was a legal sanctioning of this fact.

Now the U.S. Department of Education had done just that.

Aftermath of a Ban

WORLD VIEW

By Michael Burns

August 2, 2037

HOUSTON, Texas—This month is the two-year anniversary of the date on which a total ban on abortion had been enacted by the Congress of the United States. The latest report from Planned Parenthood showed that during these two years there were 475 arrests and convictions for illegally performed abortions in the entire country. The actual number of illegally performed abortions has been estimated to run into at least 600,000. It is instructive at this point to review the steps that led to the ban and to survey the conditions that have ensued since the ban went into effect.

In the years preceding the Supreme Court's *Kemp v. Berry* decision, the pro-choice movement had been severely weakened by adoption of state ballot initiatives that restricted abortion. Some initiatives specified mandatory pre-abortion requirements, such as a waiting period, ultrasound viewing of the fetus, or counseling by a psychologist or clergyman. Other initiatives required abortion clinics to adhere to strict and detailed building regulations and/or stipulated that the procedure had to be performed by a licensed physician in a hospital, with a clergyman of choice in attendance.

The *Kemp v. Berry* ruling of September 15, 2031, which allowed all types of religious expression by any holder of a private or public office, ended the controversy regarding the interpretation of the First Amendment of the Constitution. The ruling effectively tore down the wall of separation between church and state and led to an upsurge in religious activism that affected all aspects of people's lives, including the controversy about abortion. The ruling empowered the pro-life movement to redouble its efforts to have abortion banned entirely. In the forefront of this effort was the *Alliance for the Advancement of Christian Ethics and Family Values* , a powerful religious lobbying organization. As a first step, the *Alliance*—as it was commonly called—lobbied Congress to defund Planned Parenthood, an organization profoundly despised by the Religious Right. Defunding had been brought up in Congress before, but had not passed. But on November 9, 2032, with large Republican majorities in both houses, Congress voted to cut off all federal funding to Planned Parenthood. The vote thrilled the Religious Right, but had no effect on Planned Parenthood's abortion activity because, for many years, the organization had used federal funds solely to support its non-abortion services.

The Alliance's next move was to lobby the Supreme Court to revisit the 1973 *Roe v. Wade* decision. That ruling, long decried by the Religious Right, had specified that states could not ban abortion during the first three months of pregnancy, but that they could regulate, but not ban, abortion during the second trimester. The judges agreed to reconsider the earlier ruling and on April 12, 2034 voted to overturn it. They declared that henceforth abortion was banned and illegal throughout the country.

In order to assure that the abortion ban was ironclad, the Alliance lobbied Congress to enact into law a related item, namely the "egg-as-a-person" concept. In deliberating the new law, Congress was reviving a state ballot proposal that defined a fertilized egg as a person regardless of whether or not that egg led to formation of an embryo. The measure had first been introduced in Mississippi in 2011 and subsequently in several other states, but had failed to win support. But times had changed. On August 15, 2035, the measure was passed by Congress with overwhelming support.

*

By so doing, Congress had effectively declared abortion to be tantamount to murder and had opened the door to criminal prosecution of both the patient and the abortionist. States are now charged with enforcing the abortion ban and most have opted to delegate that responsibility to their county governments. Usually, these have charged the sheriff with enforcement of the ban. Many sheriffs have set up roaming two-men teams, which have become known as *Abortion Squads*, in order to ferret out violators. Surveillance by Abortion Squads has concentrated on Planned Parenthood clinics (even though they now provide only non-abortion services), defunct private abortion clinics, residences of doctors who had performed abortions, and red light districts and slum neighborhoods where back-alley abortions might be carried out. Abortion Squads are issued permanent search warrants that allow them free access to any private residence. Citizens are asked to call 9-1-1 if they actually witness an abortion or suspect a place where abortions might be performed.

Enforcement has been extremely effective; very few illegal abortions have been reported. Once apprehended, violators are prosecuted swiftly. A woman who desires to have an abortion has only two options. She can subject herself to a back-alley procedure which, in addition to dangers from botched surgery, carries with it the fear of being caught and taken to court. So far, the death penalty has not been invoked, but long jail sentences have certainly been meted out. The only other option is to go outside the country, perhaps to Canada or Mexico, which are the closest. Abortion traffic to those countries has increased, but the cost of making such a trip is a deterrent for many pregnant women. What has increased much more is the number of women forced to give birth to a child no matter what the circumstances. It is not known what long-term effects these unwanted pregnancies might have on the physical and mental health of the mothers and their children. Nor is it known how society-at-large—which ultimately has to deal with the financial, social, and mental issues of these mothers and their children—might be affected.

Ominous Clouds

WORLD VIEW

By Harold Nelson

November 14, 2038

BERLIN, Germany—November 9, 2038, the 100th anniversary of Kristallnacht (November 9, 1938), turned out to be, in President Roosevelt's words, a day which will live in infamy.

The 1938 pogrom against the Jews of Germany, Austria and the Sudetenland (part of Czechoslovakia) had been carried out by rampaging mobs of paramilitary forces and civilians. Authorities had looked on, but did not intervene, as coordinated deadly attacks targeted Jewish businesses, synagogues, schools, hospitals, and homes. The name Kristallnacht (Crystal Night or the Night of Broken Glass) refers to the shards of glass from smashed windows of ransacked buildings that littered the streets. The toll of the anti-Semitic pogrom was staggering. Over 1,000 synagogues were burned and over 7,000 businesses were destroyed. More than one hundred Jews were massacred, hundreds more were injured, some three hundred despaired and committed suicide, and 30,000 were arrested and sent to Nazi concentration camps.

Commemoration of the 100th anniversary of Kristallnacht did not generate quite the same horrendous statistics, but it did represent a serious re-enactment of the original pogrom. Throughout Europe, swastikas and virulent graffiti were scrawled on synagogues, Jewish businesses, and Jewish schools. Tombstones were vandalized, and the internet was flooded with hate-filled anti-Semitic diatribes. Neo-Nazi parties in France, Belgium, Hungary, and Greece organized rallies at which speakers spewed their anti-Semitic and racist venom. There were suicide bombings at Jewish-owned groceries and delicatessens in London, Brussels, Stockholm, and Oslo. An innocent-looking customer (male or female) would enter the store, mingle with the people and then blow himself/herself up. Pandemonium ensued as stunned survivors rushed for exits from blood-spattered establishments. Other murderous attacks targeted Jewish day schools in Paris, Berlin, Amsterdam, Vienna, and Rome. A car would pull up to the school while classes were still in session. The driver stayed behind as the car disgorged one or more heavily armed men who forced their way into the school, headed for the nearest classroom, sprayed the frightened students and their teacher with fire from their AK-47 assault rifles, and fled. Well over a hundred people lost their life in the attacks on stores and schools and several hundred more were wounded, many seriously. Authorities ascertained that the attackers were either Islamic radicals or neo-Nazis, and, in some cases, the two groups had coordinated their dastardly deeds.

*

How did Europe get to this point? After World War II and the horror of the Holocaust it seemed that the world had embraced a resolution of "never again." Anti-Semitism, rampant for 2,000 years, appeared to be in decline. However, much of it went simply underground. What then accounted for its re-emergence and the intensity it acquired, especially in Europe? There are several parts to the answer. The economic woes of the continent made it convenient to have a scapegoat that could be blamed for whatever problems countries were dealing with; the rise of neo-Nazis and other far-right extremist groups across Europe helped stoke the fires of anti-Jewish bigotry and prejudice; and the virulent anti-Semitic hatred emanating from the Arab world in the Middle East and from its proxy Muslim communities throughout Europe added coals to the fire.

Arguably, the most telling reason for the resurgence of anti-Semitism has been the creation of the State of Israel in 1948. At first, the young nation elicited grudging respect, but before long this turned into criticism and disparagement, which eventually became outright hatred and full-blown anti-Semitism.

*

Over 2,000 years, classical anti-Semitism generally progressed in three stages. The first was characterized by demonizing Jews (Jews are usurers, Jews poison wells, Jews spread the plague, and so on). Many of these unfounded accusations survive to this day, especially the blood libel and the *Protocols of the Elders of Zion*. The former accuses Jews of killing Christian children and using their blood in the baking of matzo, the unleavened bread eaten at Passover. The latter is an infamous forgery, first published in 1903, that purports to authenticate a supposed Jewish global conspiracy to control the world. The publication is still wide-spread and has been dramatized on television in the Arab world though long ago having been exposed as invidious fiction. Anti-Semitism's second stage led to the exclusion of Jews from the general society (forced to wear special dress, restricted to living in ghettos, allowed only into certain professions, subjected to Nazi race laws, and the like). The final stage brought on the expulsion or destruction of the Jews (such as the expulsion from Spain, Russian pogroms, and Nazi extermination camps in the Holocaust).

Modern anti-Semitism, born after the creation of the State of Israel, came with one important change. Instead of targeting Jews as individuals, it focused on Jews as a collective nation. Israel, rather than Jews in general, became the immediate object of hate and persecution. In the process, anti-Semitism became global. Previously, it had been limited largely to countries where Jews had taken up residence. Now it extended throughout the world, even to countries where not a single Jew lived, even to people who had never met a Jew. Israel became the scapegoat much as individual Jews had filled that role before and anti-Semitism world-wide now masqueraded as anti-Zionism. Regardless that modern anti-Semitism differed from previous anti-Semitism in this important aspect, it still progressed along the same classic lines.

*

In the first stage, Israel was demonized. It was criticized and condemned both privately and in the halls of governments and the United Nations. The Arab world vilified Israel in textbooks and the media. Israel was accused of being an apartheid state, its citizens compared to Nazis, its leadership called warmongers. When Hamas hid its rocket launchers in schools and hospitals and when hundreds of rockets would strike Israel, the international community was mum. However when Israel, in-self defense, responded with a retaliatory strike, the world was in an uproar. No other country had ever been held to similar standards.

In the second stage, attempts were made to exclude Israel from the body politic as much as possible. At the UN, Israel was treated as a pariah nation, subjected to bias and discrimination. For years it was blocked from bidding for a seat on the Security Council. Outside the UN, Israel was struck with economic boycotts, academic boycotts, and cultural boycotts. Divestments were initiated in which universities, companies, and religious organizations voted to withdraw their financial holdings from companies doing business in Israel. The BDS movement (boycott, divestment, sanction) encapsulates these efforts.

As of this writing, the first two stages continue to be active. Beyond those, the peril of stage three looms on the horizon. Its message has already been put into words, both verbally and in writing. Iran has repeatedly threatened to "wipe Israel off the map." In the Arab world, the PLO, Hamas, Hezbollah, and Fatah have all called for Israel's destruction, as has the rhetoric emanating from mosques around the globe.

*

This is the background against which one must view the reenactment of Kristallnacht. Many writers have pointed out, that anti-Semitism is never just about the Jews. It begins with the Jews, but never ends with them. Nazi anti-Semitism ended up engulfing the world in a horrendous war. Palestinian anti-

Semitism, through its "invention" of airline hijackings and suicide bombers, has already contributed immensely to the rise and spread of world-wide terrorism. Who knows what ramifications will come out of the current global anti-Semitism? Martin Niemoeller, a prominent Protestant pastor, had been an outspoken foe of the Nazis and had spent the last seven years of their rule in concentration camps. A speech that he gave on January 6, 1946, included the following famous lines:

> First they came for the Jews
> and I did not speak out
> because I was not a Jew.
>
> Then they came for the Communists
> and I did not speak out
> because I was not a Communist.
>
> Then they came for the trade unionists
> and I did not speak out
> because I was not a trade unionist.
>
> Then they came for me
> and there was no one left
> to speak out for me.

Rumblings in the Himalayas

WORLD VIEW

By James Morrison

May 15, 2039

NEW DELHI, India—*The Vale of Kashmir*—a magical name that evokes visions of a lush green valley studded with rice paddies, and nestled among towering snow-capped peaks—a Shangri La-like place in the Himalayas, far from the hustle and bustle of the rest of the world. At one time, the valley was known for its export of cashmere wool, the fine, soft, downy winter undercoat of cashmere goats. The valley's region has supported human civilization for thousands of years and has served as a cultural, political, and religious crossroads. The breathtaking scenery still abounds, but peace and tranquility are less in evidence ever since the region became a bone of contention between India and Pakistan, now two nuclear powers, abutting the area and claiming sovereignty over it.

Seeds of the conflict were sown on April 15, 1947, the day Britain relinquished its rule over India. For a hundred years prior to that date Kashmir had existed in India as the princely state of Jammu and Kashmir and had been governed by a Maharaja. But when Britain left, change became inevitable. India was partitioned, giving rise to the mostly Hindu Union of India (later Republic of India) and the mostly Muslim Dominion of Pakistan (later Islamic Republic of Pakistan). Since Muslims made up two thirds of Kashmir's population, it was expected that it would become part of Pakistan. However, Maharaja Hari Singh, the ruler of Jammu and Kashmir at the time, wanted his state to remain independent and refused to join either India or Pakistan. He only signed an interim "Standstill" agreement with Pakistan to maintain transport and other services. In October 1947, the Maharaja changed his mind as Pakistani tribesmen had infiltrated his state and he was fearful of being overthrown. He asked India for military assistance and signed an "Instrument of Accession" with India, ceding to it control over foreign and defense policy. Honoring his request, India airlifted troops who engaged the tribesmen in what is usually considered to have been the first India-Pakistan war (the second and third wars were fought in 1965 and 1972, respectively).

The United Nations brokered a cease-fire in 1948, by which time about two thirds of the Kashmir region was under Indian control, and became the Indian state of Jammu and Kashmir. The remaining one third of the region was under Pakistani control and became Azad (free) Kashmir. However, the cease-fire did not bring the conflict to an end. One reason for its persistence is the continuing dispute over the time-line of events in 1947. Was the Instrument of Accession signed before or after Indian troops were airlifted? Depending on the answer, the military intervention of India in Kashmir would have to be considered to have been either legal or illegal. Other reasons for the conflict continuing unabated are recurrent cross-border attacks into Jammu and Kashmir and Azad Kashmir, as well as skirmishes and terrorist acts carried out inside both India and Pakistan. All of this creates animosity, stokes distrust, and provides fodder for keeping the conflict alive. At the conclusion of the third India-Pakistan war in 1972, a "Line of Control" demarcating the area in Kashmir held by each country was agreed upon and has provided a measure of stability.

*

In addition to the political dispute, the two countries have also engaged in a conflict over the distribution of water from the Indus river. That issue arose shortly after 1947, but to the two nations' credit, it was settled in 1960. On September 19 of that year, the World Bank brokered an "Indus Water Treaty," which was signed in Karachi by Jawaharlal Nehru, India's prime minister, and Ayub Khan, Pakistan's president. Since then, both countries have siphoned off water from the Indus river and have built dams to provide for irrigation and hydroelectricity, but have done so under the terms of the treaty.

However, the water distribution issue has resurfaced in recent times (especially since 2025) and in an even more serious form than was the case originally. What both countries must now face and deal with is the fact that the amount of fresh water supplied by the Indus and its tributaries has declined significantly over the past decade due to the shrinking of the massive glaciers that feed the rivers at their origin and along the way. Essentially all scientific experts consider global warming to be the cause for the loss of glacier mass. The latter is a critical issue because most of the fresh water used by Kashmir and large parts of Pakistan comes from the Indus and its tributaries. Moreover, while the supply of this water has dwindled, demand for it has gown because of the population growth along the rivers and the drainage of water by both India and Pakistan for irrigation and hydroelectricity. Once the amount of water provided by the Indus and its tributaries falls below a critical level as it is bound to, it will be a matter of life and death for the millions who rely on it for agriculture and power.

To put this in perspective, consider what is involved. The Indus is one of the world's major rivers and has been the lifeblood for some of the largest human habitations of the ancient world dating back to about 3,000 BCE. The river originates in the Tibetan plateau near Lake Mansarova. Both the river and its tributaries are fed by the thousands of glaciers of the massive Tibetan ice fields (the third largest ice sheet formation in the world, often called the third pole), and later on by mighty glaciers at the slopes of the Karakoram range (home to K2, the world's second highest mountain). The Indus flows north through the Ladakh district of Jammu and Kashmir, heads west as it passes the foothills of the Karakoram range, and then flows south through Pakistan until it empties into the Arabian Sea near the seaport of Karachi. At that point, the Indus has traveled some 2,000 miles.

Various glacier monitoring centers have warned about the shrinkage of glaciers for many years and have stressed the grave implications of this for India and Pakistan. Beginning in 2035 these reports have taken on an ominous tone. The consensus was that the Asian glaciers had receded in recent years at an accelerated rate. The figures were extremely disconcerting. The Indian Geoscience Association, the Pakistani Institute of Glacier Research, the Chinese Tibetan Plateau Research Association, and the Himalayan Academy for Geoscience all reported that the Tibetan glaciers had lost 10% of their mass over the last ten years and that the Karakoram glaciers had lost an astonishing 18% of their length over the same time period.

Since these glaciers feed all three great rivers of the Indian subcontinent (Indus, Ganges, and Brahmaputra) as well as other rivers flowing through Cambodia, Laos, and Vietnam, their shrinkage portends a grim future for many countries. Not only India and Pakistan, but almost all of South Asia will have to contend with the decline of fresh water carried by these rivers and their tributaries, a looming water shortage that will affect the lives of more than a billion people.

*

These doomsday reports are having profound political repercussions in many Asian countries, particularly in India and Pakistan where the issue has been hotly debated by all political parties. Moreover, two new parties have been founded, one in each country, with the explicit agenda of fighting for an adequate water supply for their nation. Both parties, "Indus for India (IFI)," and "Water for Pakistan (WFP)," have taken extreme positions and are vociferous about them. Each party advocates that its country put national interest ahead of adherence to the Indus Water Treaty, which both parties claim has outlived its usefulness and has become obsolete. IFI argues that, since the Indus flows first through Indian territory before crossing into Pakistan, India should rank ahead of Pakistan in drawing upon its water. WFP argues that the number of people relying on the river's life-giving water is infinitely larger for Pakistan than it is for India. Therefore, providing for Pakistani needs should take precedence. IFI and WFP leaders have been interviewed repeatedly on radio and television, and protest marches and mass gatherings have taken place in both Delhi and Islamabad. Several IFI and WFP party officials have been dispatched to Jammu, the winter capital of Jammu and Kashmir, and to Muzaffarabad, the capital of Azad Kashmir, with the goal of organizing strong local support groups for the two parties. The looming water shortage, the founding of IFI and WFP, and the scope of their activities have all combined to inflame the political scene to such an extent that it threatens the uneasy truce between the two nuclear nations.

Additionally, the two nations' militaries have taken menacing steps by beefing up troops in and around Kashmir and by readying heavy armor as well as air and naval forces. It seems that the almost 100-year old conflict, now aggravated by the dispute over fresh water supplies is slowly, but inexorably, moving toward becoming another all-out India-Pakistan war. It does not help that the two Defense Ministers keep reiterating that "all options are on the table," thereby raising the specter of an almost unimaginable nuclear confrontation. To make matters even worse, China's Ministry of the Interior announced a few weeks ago that the government was considering diverting a portion of the glacial melt water from the Tibetan plateau to irrigate large areas of the Chinese mainland. "China has every right to use the resources located in its own backyard for the benefit of its citizens," declared the assistant to the minister. The announcement was a stark reminder that China did, in fact, have its hand on South Asia's major water spigot, thereby putting South Asia's countries at China's mercy. That realization had Ministers of Defense throughout South Asia huddle in hurriedly-convened conferences, since China's potential action in Tibet would be almost tantamount to a formal declaration of war.

In years past, wars were fought over oil and natural resources. By now, in some parts of the world, water has become the most precious commodity and its scarcity may well trigger wars.

A Nation in the Throes of Death

WORLD VIEW

By James Morrison

September 9, 2040

COLOMBO, Sri Lanka—Are the Maldive Islands destined to become a modern-day Atlantis, the legendary island that disappeared into the sea? That is the question Maldivians have been asking themselves for the last twenty-eight years.

Our knowledge of Atlantis—the "lost continent"—comes from the writings of Plato. According to Plato, Poseidon, God of the Sea, had fallen in love with Cleito, a mortal woman and the two had ten sons. Poseidon took the land on which Cleito's dwelling stood and formed it into an island, which he named Atlantis after Atlas, his first-born son. As Plato described it, an advanced civilization flourished on Atlantis and its inhabitants were happy, wealthy, and virtuous. For many years they lived by the precepts of Poseidon, but eventually they forgot their divine ancestry and became corrupt, greedy, and immoral. Poseidon decided to punish the people and brought on earthquakes and floods, causing Atlantis to sink into the ocean and disappear from sight. Plato's account has been debated for years. Had there really been an island that sank into the sea or was the account merely the stuff of legends? Today many scholars believe that Atlantis was, in fact, the ancient Greek island of Santorini and that Plato's writings refer to the powerful volcanic eruption that occurred around 1500 BCE and destroyed most of the island.

Now, Maldivians have not been worrying about an impending volcanic eruption destroying their land. What they have been worrying about, and with good reason, are the rising sea levels that threaten to flood their almost flat islands into oblivion.

*

The Maldives, officially the Republic of Maldives, is one of the most unusual countries of the world. Located in the confluence of the Indian Ocean and the Arabian Sea, some 400 miles southwest of Sri Lanka, it is an archipelago of a double chain of atolls (coral reefs enclosing lagoons). The reef of each atoll is broken up into many separate islands. All told, there are about 20 atolls and 1200 islands, of which only some 200 are inhabited. Most of the islands are tiny and all are flat, having an average ground elevation of 4 ft 11 in (that of the Netherlands, by comparison, is 37 ft). The archipelago extends 475 miles from north to south and 80 miles from east to west. The Maldives are spread over 35,000 square miles of water but have a combined land area of only 115 square miles and a population of 394,000 (2015). The

Maldives are the lowest lying country of the world, but their scenery is that of a paradise: glittering white sand beaches, sparkling cobalt-blue waters, luscious vegetation, coconut palms and breadfruit trees swaying in the wind. Not surprisingly, the economy is based on tourism and fishing.

The Maldives have been inhabited since at least the fifth century BCE and the earliest inhabitants most likely arrived from south India and Sri Lanka. The islands have been an independent sultanate for most of their history. In 1153, they adopted Sunni Islam as their state religion. From 1887 until 1965 they were a British protectorate. In 1965, the Maldives gained full independence, and in 1968 they abolished the sultanate and proclaimed their country to be a republic.

*

In 2012 Mohamed Nasheed, former Maldivian president, warned that "if carbon emissions continue at the rate they are climbing today, my country will be under water in seven years." Since then, the industrial nations of the world have done little to alter the rate of carbon emission. As a result, Nasheed's dire prophecy has come to pass, but not in 2019 as he had predicted. Instead, it arrived in 2040.

The crisis came on slowly. For some ten years (2012-2022), water levels rose an average of 0.2 inches/year. That was followed by ten years (2022-2032) of a more significant change, with waters rising an average of 1.0 inch/year. After these twenty years, the sea level had risen by a full foot and much of the beach area was already under water. Subsequently tourism dropped precipitously, depriving a large part of the population of their livelihood.

Making the situation even more critical was the fact that the water temperature has been rising as well. While much of the world kept ignoring (or denying) climate change, the water in and around the lagoons was getting warmer. By 2026 one could observe that the corals started to undergo "coral bleaching," in which the corals lose color, turn whitish, become fragile, and often die. As coral reefs kept deteriorating, the islands became more vulnerable to the ravages of storms and monsoons.

But worse was yet to come. Beginning in 2032, the sea level began to rise at an accelerated rate of about 6.3 inches/year, a thirty-fold increase over the 2012-2022 rate. As soon as it became apparent that the water was rising dramatically, President Ibrahim Khan (the current Head of State of the Maldives) made a frantic effort to garner help from the international community. He flew to New York in 2035 and addressed the General Assembly of the United Nations, where he made an impassioned appeal. "Our situation is desperate," he said. "Unless drastic measures are implemented immediately by the world's industrialized nations to reverse the climate change trend, the Maldives are going to be under water in five years. We appeal to you to forestall our demise." Unfortunately, his appeal fell on almost deaf ears. The big polluters (United States, China, Russia, and others) did not go beyond pledging modest attempts to reduce greenhouse emissions. Seeing such feeble response, rising economies (India, Brazil, Japan, and others) did not even bother to pledge any effort. In all cases, economic considerations trumped concerns for the common good.

*

A disappointed and dejected Khan returned to the Maldives and began preparing his nation for the inevitable. He mobilized the government to help the people as much as possible by setting up three new departments—*Relocation*, *Travel*, and *Compensation*. The *Relocation Department* was charged with trying to purchase land in India, Sri Lanka, and Australia for resettlement of all or some of the Maldivians. Purchases were to be paid for by contributions from both local donors and foreign sources. If successful, these resettlements would evolve into communities that would keep Maldivian history and culture alive. The *Travel Department* was charged with procuring all necessary passports, visas and other travel documents. The department was also responsible for securing air flights and sea transport for the mass exodus expected in 2040. Lastly, the *Compensation Department* was charged with helping the Maldivians financially by distributing to them the moneys accumulated in the government treasury from tourism over the past few years.

Four years later, in 2039, the water level had risen a total of 4 ft 8 in and was getting perilously close to the average height of the islands above sea level (4 ft 11 in). Once water started lapping around the country's highest points, it heralded the beginning of the end. All real estate activity ground to a halt. Current and future construction projects were abandoned. No one was interested in buying property and no one was able to sell any. Most other parts of the economy were devastated as well. Only the fishing industry continued to function.

People began to leave the Maldives. Departures were at first a mere trickle, mostly made up of the wealthiest on the islands. They usually left by air, using a special runway that had been constructed two feet above ground. As time went on, the pace of departure increased. By the spring of this year a virtual torrent of humanity was streaming toward Male, the country's capital and chief port. A motley flotilla of sea-going vessels (large fishing boats, catamarans, yachts, sailboats, freighters, and other vessels on loan from neighboring countries) was waiting there to transport the Maldivians to secure lands.

Finally, the day arrived for the last people to leave the Maldives. Much as a captain is the last to leave a sinking ship, so president Khan has opted to be the last to leave his sinking country. As dawn broke on Monday, August 27, 2040, the president and his entourage left the presidential palace, lowered all flags, and drove to the port, their cars sloshing through flooded streets. The cars were abandoned at the pier where a large presidential yacht was waiting to take on the distinguished passengers. The gangway was lowered and the president and his retinue went on board. As the yacht pulled away from the pier a small band on the upper deck played the national anthem, Qaumii Salaam (National Salute). Looking at the receding shoreline and Male's shrinking skyline, the passengers felt the bitter irony of the last stanza:

> May the State ever have auspicious honor and respect
> With good wishes for your continuing might, we salute you

With tears in their eyes, the presidential party stood on deck and saluted their sinking homeland, the place where they and their ancestors had lived since 500 BCE. It would take many years for the last vestiges of the country to disappear completely, but slowly and inexorably the man-made Maldivian civilization will be washed away. Eventually, the Maldives will become an Atlantis, albeit a modern one, of whose existence in the past there won't be a shred of doubt.

Made in the USA
Middletown, DE
25 June 2016